FALLING FOR THE NEIGHBOR NEXT DOOR

"Do you believe a person only has one soul mate, and if they miss their chance to connect with that person, they have to settle for less?" Ian asked.

Tessa blinked. Where had that come from? "I sure hope not. There are a lot of people in the world. It would be hard to find the one-and-only that was meant for you."

Ian circled the island to help her dish up their food. When his arm brushed hers, he turned and looked down at her. Her breath caught in her throat, and she couldn't back away from him. They were too close.

She gazed into his chocolate brown eyes, held by the emotion in their depths. He bent his head, and his lips grazed hers. Heat sizzled through her veins, made her nerves sing for more . . .

COOKING UP TROUBLE

A Mill Pond Romance

Judi Lynn

LYRICAL SHINE PRESS
Kensington Publishing Corp.
www.kensingtonbooks.com

LYRICAL SHINE BOOKS are published by

Kensington Publishing Corp.
119 West 40th Street
New York, NY 10018

All Kensington titles, imprints, and distributed lines are available at special quantity discounts for bulk purchases for sales promotion, premiums, fund-raising, educational, or institutional use.

Special book excerpts or customized printings can also be created to fit specific needs. For details, write or phone the office of the Kensington Sales Manager: Kensington Publishing Corp., 119 West 40th Street, New York, NY 10018. Attn. Sales Department. Phone: 1-800-221-2647.

Lyrical Shine and Lyrical Shine logo trademarks of Kensington Publishing Corp.

First Electronic Edition: April 2016
eISBN-13: 978-1-60183-783-7
eISBN-10: 1-60183-783-6

First Print Edition: April 2016
ISBN-13: 978-1-60183-784-4
ISBN-10: 1-60183-784-4

Printed in the United States of America

ACKNOWLEDGMENTS

I'd like to thank my agent, Lauren Abramo, at Dystel and Goderich for being so patient and supportive of me. Without her I never would have tried to write romance. I didn't think I could do it. She had faith in me though, and pushed me forward. I'm so happy she did.

I'd also like to thank my husband for always believing in me, whatever I try. And my daughters Holly and Robyn. Holly reads all of my roughest work and steers me in the right direction. Robyn's the best cheerleader a mother could have.

I'd also like to thank Mary Lou Rigdon (who writes Regencies as Julia Donner) and Ann Staadt for being my trusted critique partners. They catch almost everything. And Paula Adams for prodding me to always add layers to my characters.

And thanks to my sisters Mary and Patty Thompson, who take me out to eat when I'm in a funk. And to Heidi Gatto who's the best "adopted" daughter anyone could want.

Chapter 1

Buck Krieger was busy with another customer, so Tessa finished loading the last of the blueberry bushes into her old, beat-up pickup alone. She rubbed her lower back. Before making the drive here, one town over, she'd dug the holes for each and every bush, and her muscles felt it. The new patch was going in the long, rectangular plot on the east side of her property, right after the strawberry beds.

A breeze whipped strands of her tangled, coppery hair across her face. She scraped them behind her ears. She'd used the new, fancy combs her mother had sent her, but they couldn't tame her thick, wild locks. She'd given up and tossed the combs into her purse. That's what she got for trying to look feminine when she was doing outdoor work.

Her mom would be disappointed. Mom tried, bless her, sending make-up kits, wrapped in pearly pink paper, and certificates for facials or manicures. If Mom saw her fingernails this spring, she'd die of heart failure. Dirt rimmed every one of them. It was impossible to keep them clean when she worked in the gardens every day. That wasn't even the worst of it. Mom would sit on her and smear sunscreen on her face if she saw the new sprinkle of freckles that peppered her nose and cheeks.

Bushes loaded, Tessa started down the narrow, nursery drive slow and easy. Winter had washed enough gullies in the gravel to make for a bumpy ride. She'd paid in advance, but Buck still stopped her to say his goodbyes. "You already have plenty of blueberries for jams. These are for pies, right?"

Tessa smiled and nodded. The man loved his pies. When she'd

inherited her grandparents' small farm, it came with plenty of orchards and berry patches, and he'd become a steady customer.

Buck leaned against her truck for a short chat. "People were in here, asking about you earlier today. Thought they'd drive out to your place and look you up."

"I didn't see anyone. I wasn't at the house, though. I was working on my berry beds. Did you get their names?"

"Ann and Rich York. Seemed like nice folks."

She couldn't hide her surprise. No, make that worry. Why would they look her up? Gary's parents had always been kind to her, welcomed her into their lives with open arms when Gary took her home to meet them. She gulped a deep breath.

Buck frowned. "Guess it's a good thing you missed them."

Tessa squared her shoulders. "They're my ex's mom and dad. Nice as can be, but I don't need the memories." It had been three years since she'd walked into Gary's apartment and found Sadie in his arms. Three years since she'd taken off her engagement ring and hurled it at him. He'd called out to her when she stomped down the stairs, but what was there to say? It was over. Done.

Buck nodded. "Some things are best left in the past."

She forced a smile. "Well, these bushes aren't going to plant themselves. I'd better get going."

Buck backed away from the pickup. His expression said he was sorry he'd ruined her day, but how could he know?

When she reached the country road at the end of Buck's drive, she turned left toward her white bungalow and the acres it sat on. She'd turned the barn in the side yard into a farm stand and bakery. She closed the stand each winter and didn't reopen until the first of May, two and a half weeks away, but she sold baked goods all year 'round on Fridays and Saturdays with special requests available by order.

She was halfway home, flying past farm fields, when she saw a sleek, black car parked on the side of the road. A dark-haired, lanky man stood beside it, waving his arms to get her attention. He wore a suit and black shoes that gleamed in the sunlight. She pulled up beside him and rolled down her window.

"I'm in a jam," he said. "My car has a flat, and I'm not sure where I am, so I can't give directions to get help."

He was damned good-looking. Not gorgeous, but easy on the

eyes. She didn't trust him already. Good-looking men would eventually cheat. Women threw themselves at them, and they caved after time, succumbed to temptation. She had to give this guy credit, though. He didn't try the charm or smiles that most handsome men used, and she was sure it would work for him. He looked to be about six-four with black hair and brown eyes. *Off-limits.*

Tessa frowned. "Do you have a spare?"

He raised his eyebrows and shrugged. "The car's a rental. I'm not sure."

Tessa got out of her pickup. "Let's look in the trunk. Mill Pond's only a few miles away. A donut'll get you there. You can get a new tire and be on your way."

He unlocked the trunk and pointed at the empty space. "See? Nothing's there."

Tessa blinked at him and shook her head. She flipped up the dark mat and pointed to the wheel well with its spare and jack.

A blush rose to his cheeks and he pressed his lips together. "I live in New York. Don't own a car, always use public transit. I've never changed a tire."

Tessa shrugged. "I've changed plenty of them. I own a farm. Something's always breaking down. Give me a hand."

He tried. He really did, but he was pretty much useless. He stood with his arms crossed over his chest as she changed the tire. When she finished, he said, "Let me pay you for your help. I appreciate your rescuing me."

Tessa laughed. "Not exactly a rescue. Your life wasn't in danger, and someone else would've come along."

"I still appreciate it." He pulled out a wallet and riffled through the bills.

"We don't do things that way around here. When we offer help, it's because it's the right thing to do. You might want to stop in town for a new tire, though. You don't want to drive too long on a spare. Try Garth's Gas Station. He's good at repairs and won't overcharge you."

"Thanks. The place I'm going to is close to Mill Pond." He put his wallet away and narrowed his eyes, studying her. "Do you live around here?"

"Orchard Knoll." She wiped her hands on her jeans. The dirt from the tire joined the dirt from her gardening. "My property bumps up against the east side of the lake."

He stared. "I think you may border *my* property—Lakeview Stables. I closed on it last month, and I'm finally ready to move in and get it running."

"You're the new owner?" Tessa and Ned Cooper, a Mill Pond old-timer, were two of the few people in Mill Pond who didn't have something bad to say about Sam Dramer, who'd lived there previously. Sam complained about anything and everything, constantly causing a ruckus, but Tessa's jams and baked goods had won him over. And Ned had known him since they dipped fishing lines together when they played hooky from grade school.

He held out his hand. No calluses. Definitely a city boy. "Ian McGregor." A smile lit up his face. "I guess we're neighbors."

"Tessa Lawrence. Are you on your way to your property now?"

He nodded.

"Then follow me. I'll take you to Garth's station and then drive you to your place." She got in her old pickup. "It's been empty for a month now. Are you staying there?"

"I hired people to get one room on the ground floor ready for me. Then I can oversee when the crews come to clean and paint the interior. I'm making it into a lodge."

She'd heard that. It would be the perfect property with a wide expanse of beach and rolling, green horse pastures.

"Would you like to see it?" he asked. "I've heard the former owner hardly ever invited anyone inside."

She smiled. "Sam and I got along fine. I bribed him with fresh treats and jams."

His eyebrows shot up in surprise. "You must be the woman who runs the farm stand and bakery."

"Yup, that's Orchard Knoll." Before she thought about it properly, she said, "If your car's not finished in time for supper, you could stop by my place. Feel free."

"Okay, what time?" He accepted faster than she'd expected. It was a neighborly thing to do, to invite him, but she didn't really think he'd take her up on it.

"Is six okay?" She'd already put the roast and vegetables in the slow-cooker and she'd baked a pie before she left the house.

"I'll be there."

Damn. He might seem like a nice guy, but he probably wasn't. She'd invited him, though, and she couldn't take it back. With a nod, she got in her pickup and motioned for him to follow her. She led him to Garth's garage, waited for him to explain his problem, and then she drove him to Lakeview Stables.

He inhaled a deep breath when he saw the place. Built of flagstone, the central building stood three stories high with two long wings branching off of it. White trim set off the stonework, and a red tin roof matched the red double doors at its entrance. It was one fine-looking place—outside. Nothing had been done to it inside since Sam's wife died twelve years ago.

Ian shook his head. "It's as beautiful as I remember when I came to inspect it."

Tessa noticed the fallen branches that dotted the yard and the overgrown bushes. "This place could use some love again. I'm glad you bought it."

"Come with me to see if the key works? I'd hate to be stranded out here."

City folks. If buildings didn't bump up against each other, they didn't feel comfortable. She got out of the pickup and pointed across the tall grass in the paddocks toward the direction of her property. "My place is over there."

"How far?" He frowned at the vast spaces that surrounded him. The front yard faced the country road, and the back of the property rolled down to meet the lake. The paddocks sprawled on one side, and an overgrown field sprawled on the other. Rumor was he was going to make that property into some kind of fancy golf course and add tennis courts at the back some place. Plus, add horses for riders.

"Sam had to use a golf cart to get to his mailbox and back before he moved. It's in the barn. Drive that over. This road's not busy, at least, not yet."

"Not yet?" He turned to frown at her.

She shook her head. "Everyone here's expecting a lot more traffic once your place gets popular."

His frown deepened. "Does that bother you?"

"It'll take some getting used to, but everything changes, doesn't it? It's part of life."

"I guess so. This has been my dream for a long time, owning a resort." He opened the front door and took a step inside the house. "It's not as dusty as I expected it to be."

"Iris Clinger hired Luther to clean it up a bit."

Ian sighed and ran a hand through his dark hair. "Luther?"

"The boy who works for me summers and on Saturdays all year. A hard worker. Don't get any ideas. He's mine." She didn't add that Luther was the moodiest kid she'd ever met and you had to understand grunts to communicate with him.

Ian turned his warm brown eyes on her. They looked almost golden in the center. "Does everyone know everyone else around here?"

She laughed. "It's a small community. If you fart in your front yard and the wind's blowing east, your neighbor will be talking about it the next time you see him."

He blinked. "I'll try to wait till the wind's blowing toward the lake."

She shook her head. "No good, the wind usually blows to shore. You'll have to wait a long time."

He stared at her a minute, then threw back his head and laughed. "I get it. Everyone knows your dirty laundry here."

"Pretty much."

"Then I'd better learn to be discreet."

She raised her eyebrows. "Hmm, that much to hide? This should be interesting."

With a grin, he motioned for her to follow him as he toured the first floor of the house. A small room, near the back, had a double bed made up and ready. He went to the kitchen and opened a few cupboards. A bag of ground coffee sat in the one above the coffee pot. "No food, but I can figure that out later."

"No problem. When you come to my place for supper, I'll send you home with some leftovers and a coffee cake for breakfast."

He turned and reached for her hand. "Thank you. You've been really nice. It's made this easier."

She felt a blush creep up her neck and stain her cheeks. "We're neighbors. It's what country neighbors do."

"Well, I appreciate it. If you ever need any help, let me know."

She couldn't hide her surprise.

He glowered. "I might not be good with tools, but I'm good at finances, business, things like that."

"So am I, but thanks for the offer."

He stared. "You're good at money management, too?"

"I took accounting before I dropped out of college."

He thought a minute. "If you need a spider killed, a hand held, I'm your man."

He was pretty sweet, really. But Gary had been sweet, too. Nice, handsome men might make great friends, but nothing more. "I'll keep that in mind. For now, I've got to go. I have blueberry bushes to plant. You have a beautiful place. Settle in and I'll see you at six."

With a nod, he watched her go.

On the drive home, she couldn't help thinking about him. Boy, did he have a lot to learn. She'd been lucky. She'd stayed with her grandparents every summer before she'd moved here. She knew what to expect of a small town. She had a feeling Ian McGregor didn't have a clue.

Chapter 2

Tessa spent the next few hours planting her new bushes. The knees of her jeans were caked with dirt, her cheeks were smudged, and she looked a mess. But by the time Ian knocked on her front door, she'd showered and changed. She wore her good jeans and a long sleeved, cream-colored T-shirt. Once the sun set, the air turned cool. She let her hair dry naturally, flowing around her shoulders, which meant it curled every which way.

When she opened the front door for him, he held out a bottle of wine before he entered the house. He stared at her. "You have gorgeous hair."

She laughed. "Thanks, come in." Men always noticed her hair. It was flattering, but nothing more.

Ian stepped into the foyer, stopped to soak in his surroundings, and then sighed. "This place feels so homey, cozy. I'd like to get that feel at the lodge."

"Lived-in. My grandparents owned it before they gave it to me."

She led him toward the kitchen at the back of the house, but he kept getting sidetracked to look at things. "I didn't realize bungalows were this spacious."

She shook her head. "This is a wide one."

"With a big, inviting porch. The lodge needs a bigger porch." He glanced out the front window at the wicker furniture. Then he studied the arches that connected the living room to the kitchen and the side hallway. "How many bedrooms?"

"Two down, two up."

"Nice. The lodge is bigger. Do you think I could make it feel warm like this?"

"Let's talk about it over supper. Everything's ready. When we're finished, I'll give you a tour of the place."

"I'd like that." He grinned. His grin was good. A girl could be swayed if she wasn't careful.

He sighed again when they walked through the arch into the kitchen. White cupboards lined three walls. One row had glass panels to show off the dishes, bowls, and crockery inside. Granite counter tops provided plenty of workspace. Oak floors gleamed in the sunlight spilling through the windows. He sniffed the air. "I wish Lily liked to cook."

"Lily?"

He jammed his hands into his jeans pockets, embarrassed. "My fiancée. I came here to get things ready, and then she's going to join me."

"Smart girl, she'll miss all the dust and mess."

Ian frowned at her. "I should have told you about Lily sooner. I wasn't thinking. If you cooked a meal to impress me . . ."

Tessa snorted. "Sorry, I'm not looking. I invited you over because you're my neighbor. I'm glad you're engaged. Now we don't have that awkward guy-girl thing to worry about."

Color tinged his cheeks. "I sounded like an ass, didn't I? But girls have invited me for home-cooked meals before, hoping—"

She cut him off. "I get it. No problem."

His shoulders relaxed. "We can be friends?"

"That's my limit these days." She motioned him to a seat at the cherry table and went to carry the food over. "Why don't you pour us some of that wine?"

His gaze scanned the area, the French doors that led out to a three-season room and the white picket fence that bordered the small yard beyond that. Flowerbeds circled the fence, new shoots just beginning to sprout. An herb garden grew at the corner by the house. Beyond the private yard was a vista of gardens and trees, all leading to the lake.

"Where's your bakery?" he asked. "In town?"

She dished chuck roast, potatoes, carrots, onions, and celery onto his plate, then filled her own, then passed him the sautéed green beans. "No, there's a breezeway that leads to the garage. It blocks the view of the barn on that side of the property. That's where the farm stand and bakery are."

"So you never have to leave your property, if you don't want to."

"I'm not very social, but being around people is nice now and then. It's convenient having everything close, though. I spend a lot of time in the barn and gardens in good weather."

He looked up from his plate, frowning. "And in bad weather? What do you do then?"

She grimaced. "I write."

He almost dropped his fork. "Sorry, you just surprised me. Mill Pond doesn't look like a mecca of literary events."

She felt her eyebrow rise. Her Gramps used to call it her school-teacher look, not that she'd ever taught. "What are you saying, that only big cities have people who read?"

He gripped his fork and stumbled for a reply. "That didn't come out right. But when I think of publishing, I guess I think of New York."

"Not every writer in the whole freaking country lives there."

He threw up a hand in surrender. He looked pretty darned attractive, contrite. "True. You're a writer, and you live here. So what do you write?"

She hesitated.

He leaned forward, curious. "Porn?"

"Oh, my God!"

He leaned back in his chair and laughed. "I wish you could see your face. Priceless."

"You just said that to throw me." She jabbed her fork at him. "You're more evil than you look."

"I've heard that before. My big brother claims I was a terror. If you meet him, don't believe him." He cleared his throat, grew more serious. "I bet you're a technical writer of some kind. I know, a master gardener. No, maybe a baker." He clicked his fingers together. "Cookbooks! I bet you do cookbooks."

"Romances."

He coughed, took a sip of water, then stared. "Really? I got the impression you're not fond of—"

She interrupted. "I have lots of men friends."

"But that's not romance, is it?" He blinked, trying to organize his thoughts. "Wait. I get it. You got hurt, didn't you? And now you write about romance, because you can create your own happy endings."

She laid down her fork. Her throat dry, she looked away from him.

"Oh, crap, I'm an idiot. I didn't mean that. I don't know what's wrong with me today. I'm babbling about things I don't know. Don't pay any attention to me. Please. I'm not usually this stupid."

Tessa raised an eyebrow. "Gary happened a long time ago. I'm over it, but I've decided that fantasy is lots better than reality when it comes to relationships."

"I get it. I really do." He looked pained. "I'm guessing you've been told this over and over again, but you're an awesome cook."

It was her turn to blink. What an unsubtle change of topic. But it worked for her. She inhaled a deep breath. "I've actually started a cookbook, but it's mostly to entertain myself."

"Oh, you'd have a good one. And you have the credentials to go with the recipes. I could see yours being a success."

They went on to talk about his grandmother's corned beef and cabbage, Irish recipes, and Midwest cooking.

"But I thought McGregor would be Scottish," Tessa said.

Ian smiled. "My great-grandfather was Scottish, but my great-grandma was Irish."

Then they meandered into discussing her business and his dreams for Lakeview Stables. They both made an effort to keep the conversation steered to safe topics.

After large slices of apple pie, she took him on a tour of her house and property. When she unlocked the barn and led him into its stainless steel, commercial kitchen, he let out a low whistle. "This looks pretty serious."

"It is serious. Grandma and I make a lot of pies and jams, pestos, pickled vegetables . . ." She raised an eyebrow at him. "Right up your alley. All kinds of baked goods. We make one specialty cake and pie a week, all year round. People buy them ahead to freeze."

He turned in a slow circle in the large, front sales room. A glass case lined one wall. Empty now, but filled with pies and cakes on weekends. Wood tables of different shapes and sizes, scattered here and there, held their jams and jellies, but his attention focused on the shelves on one entire wall that were dedicated to pickling—vegetables, sauerkraut, beets, and onions, as well as every way to pickle cucumbers she and Grams could think of.

He blinked. "That's a lot of pickles."

"Not close to enough. They're one of our best sellers."

"Really." The thought clearly amazed him. His gaze scanned the store. "Would you be interested in supplying anything for the lodge's dining room once I get the business up and going?"

"We can talk about that later. I'd have to hire someone else if you'd need a lot, but you can get a lot of artisan goods around here. Carl Gruber raises grass-fed beef." She nodded to the property on the other side of hers. "Evan Meyers raises goats and is known for his milk and cheeses. The Danzas raise free-range chickens, ducks, and geese. Pheasants and rabbits, in season."

He stared. "I knew this area was known by foodies, but I didn't know there were so many options."

"We offer a lot. There's a vineyard on the north side of town." She couldn't help the note of pride that crept into her voice. Ian *had* lucked into a prime food area. As she led him back to the house and kitchen, he pointed to a small cabin that sat between her place and his. "What's that?"

"When my grandpa got older, he hired a farmhand, part-time, who worked for room and board. No one uses it now."

He studied it. "I've been thinking about building rental cabins close to the lake."

"It wouldn't be that hard." Once inside, she put their leftover supper in plastic containers to send home with him. She gave him a coffee cake from her freezer, too.

He licked his lips. Sensual lips, she noticed, that curled up on the sides. "Streusel. I love it."

"Good, then you should have a decent start tomorrow morning." Tessa waved him off as his golf cart zipped down the road and turned, out of sight. Then she went to the kitchen to finish cleaning up. She felt restless, ill at ease. Ian had brought up memories and decisions she'd pushed aside for a later date. That date had never come. And Gary's parents had stopped at Buck Krieger's, asking about her. She didn't let herself think about them, or Gary, or men. Now wasn't the right time.

Chapter 3

Early every Thursday, Tessa's grandmother drove to the farm to help bake. When Gramps died, Grams already had a plan. She signed the farm over to Tessa, gave a chunk of money to Tessa's brother, Craig (who didn't need it, he was rich enough), and Grams still had plenty of money to move into a ranch-style house in town. She didn't miss the farm, but she did enjoy spending time with Tessa. And it was mutual. They spent the day in the barn, mixing up cake batters and rolling out pie dough.

"Heard the new guy came to town." Grams had to raise her voice to be heard over the food processor, as Tessa grated carrots for this week's special. "Seen him yet?"

Tessa scraped the grated carrots into her cake batter and added cans of crushed pineapple. "I picked him up on the side of the road. He had a flat tire. Got the spare on for him, then had him follow me to Garth's before I drove him to his place."

Grams stopped crumbling cold butter into flour for her piecrusts. She stared. "The man can't change a tire?"

"He grew up in New York. Doesn't own a car. He's looking for one this weekend. I recommended a pickup."

Grams cocked her head to one side. Some women grew softer with age. She wasn't one of them. She grew leaner. With her steel gray hair, she didn't look the cuddly sort. "Sounds like you've already gotten friendly."

"Ian didn't have a car or any groceries when I drove him home, so I invited him for supper. He's been coming every night this week until he settles in."

"Do you like him?" Grams always got straight to the point.

"He's going to make a good neighbor. And he's engaged. Had you heard that?" Grams knew enough people, she was usually on top of every tidbit of information floating around Mill Pond.

"Oh." Her shoulders drooped. Obviously, she hadn't heard. "It's been a long time since you've been interested in anyone."

"It's not gonna happen. I'm happy doing what I'm doing. I don't need complications."

"Your grandpa was a complication, for sure." A grin. "That man could annoy a saint, but Lord, I loved him."

"You two were perfect for each other." Tessa turned on the mixer to start the cream cheese frosting. Maybe if there was enough noise, Grams would let the subject drop.

"Not every man's like Gary. Not all of them are rotters."

Tessa sighed. "I lost three years of my life playing at romance. I'm not wasting time on it again."

Grams divided her dough into slabs to wrap in plastic wrap. The first batch was already in the refrigerator, chilling. "Who said anything about romance? How about a little toss in the hay? Something to get the juices going again."

Tessa laughed. "My juices are just fine, thank you. Leave it alone. Give me some town dirt. You usually have something fun to talk about when we get together."

"Leona Jackson's back in town. Have you heard?"

"No." Tessa turned the mixer off. Leona had kept the town in gossip for years before she ran off with a tourist four months ago. Everyone missed her. She was the best hairdresser in Mill Pond. "Tell me about it."

Grams gave a naughty smile. "It's not like we're just gossiping, you know. You can consider this research for your books."

That was stretching it, but if it made her feel better about spilling all the dirty details, Tessa would go with it. "Did her guy come back with her?"

"What do you think? Who'd stay with that girl if he didn't have to?"

"Did she lose any clients this time?" Silly question. She was probably booked solid for a month so that everyone could hear the scoop. Leona could attract men, but she couldn't keep them. Tessa winced. Maybe people said the same thing about her.

As if reading her thoughts, Grams shook her head. "It's not like that with you, kid. You had one disaster, and you quit. But life isn't that easy."

"It is if you decide to stay single." Tessa opened the doors on their four-story ovens and slid two, oversized cake pans into each one.

"Have you heard from your mother? She's thinking about coming for a visit in June."

Finally. A serious change of subject. "Is she planning on staying a while?"

"You know your mom. She and your dad are stopping on their way out east. She thought she could squeeze us into a few days of their schedule, though."

Tessa laughed. That was her mom! Always on the go, always busy. No one could keep up with her. Since Grams had moved into a ranch house in town, she volunteered almost every day of the week, but Mom kept busy with one social event after another. As an aerobics and fitness instructor, she was well known at the tennis club, on the golf course, and at the country club. Lunches and committee meetings filled her calendar. Dad, an engineer, joked that he had to make an appointment with her, or he'd never see her.

Their talk turned to friends and family. By the end of the day, when they loaded all of the glass shelves in the shop's case, their feet hurt, and they were talked out.

Grams pecked Tessa's cheek when she turned to leave. "See you tomorrow. I expect we'll be busy. The warmer the weather, the more people want to be out and about."

Tessa locked the barn up behind them and took her time, crossing to the house. Snowdrops were blooming in the bed under the flowering crabapple tree. Hints of green waited to burst open on the Norwegian maple. A black squirrel chattered at her from one of its branches. It wanted a peanut from the nearby hanger.

She was just entering the back door when her cell phone buzzed. She glanced at the number and smiled. Ian. He was coming for an easy supper. They'd made it at seven since Tessa would be in the barn's kitchen all day. He'd offered to take her out to eat for all of the meals she'd fed him, but she knew she'd be tired. All she wanted to do for half an hour was put her feet up and watch mindless TV.

She answered the call. "Yes?"

"Hey, Tessa, could you do me a favor and call a handyman to come to my house immediately?" Ian sounded frazzled, out of sorts. "I can't get to a phone book, and I'm in a bit of a jam."

She waited. "Is everything all right?"

"Everything's fine." She doubted that. His voice was strained. Something was wrong. "Nothing I can't handle."

Oh, boy, what had he gotten himself into? She knew he'd had a crew come to work on plumbing today. They were going to put up a new glass door for his shower. She frowned. What could go wrong with that? She tried to keep her tone light. "What do you need help with?"

"A little heavy lifting." She heard a loud grunt, followed by, "Gotta go!"

She stared at the phone. What the hell? He was in trouble, but didn't want to ask for her help. Why? But that grunt had sounded desperate. She dialed Luke's number. No one picked up. She tried Garth. No one home. She grabbed the keys to her truck and drove to his place. When she knocked, no one answered. She pushed, and the door opened. She stuck her head in and called, "Is anyone home?"

Nothing. But the golf cart was parked in the drive. He hadn't gone anywhere. Had something fallen on him? Had he passed out? She walked farther into the house. "Ian?"

A muffled noise came from the bathroom. Wasn't that one of the rooms where the most home accidents happened? She hurried down the hallway. "Ian!"

"I can't hold it much longer."

"Hold what?" She knocked on the door, and it opened. Her jaw dropped, and she stared.

"Oh, God, close your eyes!" Poor Ian had his body pressed against the glass of the sliding shower doors, his knuckles white with the effort to hold the entire piece in place. One false move and the whole thing would crash to the floor and glass would go everywhere.

She tore her gaze away from awesome nakedness and glanced at his clothes, folded on top of the toilet tank. His jeans hung half-on, half-off. He'd obviously reached for them, taken his cell phone from the pocket, and then lost his grip on the shower doors.

She tried not to notice the tanned skin and taut muscles that strained against the glass. A six-pack, maybe eight. *My, oh my.* She especially tried not to let her gaze roam farther south, but she was only human. And oh goodness, *every* part of Ian was impressive, smashed against the glass. Lots better than her bakery showcase. She cleared her throat. "Can I help?"

He jerked, and she was worried he'd lose his grip on the metal frame, but he tightened his fingers and said, "If you could slide a couple of chairs close to the tub, I think we can scoot the whole thing on those for support."

She ran to grab two kitchen chairs, and with some grunts and finagling, they got the doors balanced on them and leaned the glass unit against the sidewall. Ian grabbed a towel the minute he could let go of the doors and wrapped it snugly around his waist. Even then, the man's body proved a distraction. How could he be so fit when he was clearly not an outdoorsman?

He ran a hand through his damp hair. "I'm sorry. I didn't know who else to call. I didn't mean for you to come. I didn't want you to see . . . well, what you saw."

"I called around, but couldn't get anybody." Tessa should glue her eyes shut so her gaze didn't roam to the gap the towel didn't cover in back. Ian had a great ass.

He sighed, frustrated. "The work crew came from out of town. The doors were supposed to be solid, but when I tried to get out of the tub, the whole thing started to fall on me. They'd have never gotten back in time. I can't believe you had to see me buck naked."

Had to? She'd have paid the price of admission—even if she had to break her piggy bank. Tessa had to force her gaze to stay on his face. He was so upset, she felt sorry for him, but his muscular torso deserved another look. She shrugged, trying to play off the situation. "It's no big deal." Nervous laughter spilled out before she could stop it. "I've seen a naked man before. I have an older brother, and I was engaged for three years. I won't die of shock."

His broad shoulders relaxed. Oh, lordy, it was getting steamy in here. Or maybe it was just her. Tessa had to get away from him, at least until he got some clothes on. She started toward the great room, Ian close behind her, when she stopped so suddenly, he ran into her. She'd have fallen over if he hadn't reached out to grab her.

"Tessa?" His worried look darted from her face to what she was looking at.

A petite, curvy woman jutted out her hip and raised a blonde eyebrow.

"Oh, lord. Lily! It's not what you think! My shower doors—"

She cut him off. Her blue eyes danced with amusement. "I can't leave you alone for one minute, Ian McGregor, before you get yourself in trouble."

Ian's entire face flushed brick red. He stammered, then sputtered, "I was in the shower when the glass doors started to fall. Tessa tried to call for help, but had to come over to rescue me herself."

Lily's lips curved into a smile as she held out a hand to Tessa. Dimples came and went. "Thanks for saving my beau here. I've never met a man who can find trouble like he does."

Tessa smiled, too. Would she have handled this situation so well? *Hell, no.* "Ian talks about you all the time. He's waiting for the day this place is ready so you can move in with him."

Lily turned to survey the room. "It's clean and painted. That's a start."

Gripping his towel firmly, Ian said, "Tessa volunteered to help me decorate. I love her house, and she knows where to find good antiques for our place."

Our place. Tessa hoped Lily realized how lucky she was. Ian lived, breathed, and adored his fiancée.

Lily waved away his plans and said, "I can only stay till Saturday afternoon. I have to drive to the city to be at the airport early Sunday morning. So you don't have much time to show me around." Her eyebrow rose as she looked him up and down. "You might want to get dressed first."

Ian hesitated and turned to Tessa. "Do you mind if I stand you up for supper tonight? I didn't know Lily was coming."

Lily gave a playful tug on his towel. "I wanted to surprise you."

"It's a great surprise." Tessa started to the door. "I've worked all day, and I'm beat. I'm going to grab some leftovers and veg in front of the TV."

"I owe you," Ian called after her.

"We're neighbors. It's what we do." She heard Lily's charming laugh on her way to her pickup. How wonderful it must be to feel that secure in a man's love. Lily had never once worried when she saw Ian, in a towel, trailing behind Tessa. Her mind tried to push away the image of Gary, locked in a clinch, with Sadie. There'd been no mistaking what they were up to.

She climbed into her pickup and started the engine. She leaned back against the seat for a second and squeezed her eyes shut. Maybe Grams was right. Not every man was like Gary. But after the hurt of his betrayal subsided, she had to admit that wasn't her only worry.

She'd been with Gary for their first three years of college. He

swore he loved everything about her. And when Grandma had offered her the farm, he'd encouraged her to go for it, to follow her
dreams. When he graduated in one year, he'd follow her. It had all
sounded good on paper, so she'd happily dropped out of college to
do what truly inspired her. Gary would join her later, and they'd
make Orchard Knoll their home.

Tessa shifted the truck into drive and started for her place. It was
like Ian and Lily were exactly what she and Gary could have been.
The similarities practically smacked her in the face. Tessa had tried
to surprise Gary, too. When the weather had turned bad that first year
she'd taken over the farm, Tessa had locked up everything and driven
back to St. Louis. She'd knocked on Gary's door without warning,
hoping for a happy reunion. Well, that's not the way things had
worked. No happy surprise, no sirree. Instead, there was only shock,
humiliation, and hurt. Lots of hurt.

But the real doubts and fears didn't come until later. Then, she had
to wonder. Maybe she wasn't special enough to keep a man's interest.
After all, the minute Gary graduated, he married Sadie. Tessa's mom
sent her the announcement in the newspaper. And according to any
news she got from home, Gary and Sadie were living happily ever
after. Sadie, obviously, had something she didn't. And that worried
her. Maybe she wasn't *enough*. Maybe the same thing would happen
with every man she met.

She pulled into her driveway and parked in the garage. She took a
deep breath and let out the old pain and confusion with a whoosh.
Perhaps if she used the beauty products her mom sent. Maybe if she
wore more dresses and ribbons. But she was what she was, and she
had no desire to fake it. She'd rather be alone than pretend to be
someone she wasn't. She'd be found out eventually, anyway. So why
risk it?

Chapter 4

Fridays were always busy. This one had been busier than usual. Good temperatures brought more customers. People drove from other towns to shop at the bakery. When she and Grams locked up the barn, Grams headed straight for home. "Have to rest up for tomorrow."

Tessa walked to the house and opened her refrigerator door to stare at leftovers. Nothing looked appealing. Ian was with Lily tonight. It had never bothered her to eat by herself before, but it felt lonely now. She wrinkled her nose, tossed a hot dog in the microwave, and flicked on the TV. She flipped through channels while she ate, couldn't find anything that interested her, and reached for the newest Ilona Andrews novel. A few hours later, when she couldn't keep her eyes open any more, she called it an early night.

Before Tessa opened the barn on Saturday morning, Luther showed up for work. She walked outside with him and got him started on the huge beds for lettuces. Greens could take cool temperatures and thrived in early spring. The boy, as usual, said as little as possible. He'd never win any prizes for charm, but seemed even moodier than usual. She thought he'd be in a decent mood today, since he was going to graduate on schedule a month from now. He hated school, always threatened to drop out, and she always encouraged him to stick it out. She told him she'd do cartwheels through her strawberry patches if he managed somehow. But he obviously didn't feel the joy she did.

He'd already broached the subject of working full time for her, for as long as she could use him. Easy to do in the growing seasons. Not so easy once the snow fell. But she meant to line up something else for him by then. She'd ask everyone she knew if she had to.

After she left Luther, she joined Grams behind the counter of the bakery.

"How's Luther?" Grams asked when Tessa took her place at the second cash register.

"Grumpier than usual. I thought he'd be happier, since he's almost out of school, but I thought wrong."

Grams gave a knowing nod. "Real life's staring him in the face. He's always told us he wants to move out and be on his own, but that takes money for rent and bills. It takes a full-time job."

"I can't offer him that. I can keep him busy seven months out of the year, but things slow down at the end of October. I think something's bothering him. You should talk to him. You two have a special connection."

Most people avoided Luther, considered him a pain, but Grams liked the kid. She saw something in him that other people missed.

Grams reached inside the glass case and removed one of the smaller red velvet cakes. She carried it to their tiny office, out of sight. "We'll use that to bribe him. That boy can be had by anything chocolate."

"Why not? It's worth a shot."

They didn't have time to discuss anything else. The first customer walked through the doors and from then on, customers just kept coming. By the time they turned the sign to CLOSED at five-thirty, the glass case was empty. Shelves sat half full, and Tessa knew she'd have to dig in her cellar to restock the pickles and jams, but that could wait until Monday.

She and Grams cleaned up shop and closed out the cash register, and locked the money in the safe in the office. Then Grams took the cake to the kitchen at the back of the barn. "Get the kid," she told Tessa.

Tessa pulled on a sweater to find Luther. The end of April could be fickle. A breeze had blown up in the afternoon and the air had turned chilly. Luther was covering the last row of lettuce seeds with dirt, so she waved to him. "Grams put the kettle on. She saved us a cake. Meet us in the kitchen and we'll make plans for what you should do next Saturday."

Luther scowled, but started to put away his tools. The boy had dirty blond hair, gray eyes, and sinewy muscles. Rumors were he usually won in a fight.

Tessa didn't wait on him. She went back to the kitchen and sank onto one of the island stools. Grams had three cups of coffee, lined up, ready to go. Three paper plates and forks waited for slices of the cake sitting on the granite counter. Tessa had finished her cup of coffee and was pouring herself another when Luther opened the door and closed it behind him.

Grams watched him hover just inside the building. "What's the problem? Do you need a quick getaway? Or can you sit with us a minute?"

Luther grimaced. "Am I in trouble?"

"No." Grams cut the cake and laid a slice on his plate. She put it on the counter by the stool on the end.

"Are you firing me? Did you find someone who'll work cheaper?"

"No." Grams poured him a cup of coffee and added lots of cream. She knew the boy's tastes.

He fidgeted. "Then why do you want to talk to me?"

Tessa never kept him after he finished his jobs on Saturdays. She didn't realize it would make him nervous.

"Tessa thinks something's bothering you. Is it?" Yup, just like Grams, getting straight to the point.

Luther sighed. "I gotta get more money. I could use some insurance."

Tessa heard the desperation in his voice. She frowned. "A new owner bought Lakeview Stables. He's buried in odd jobs. Have you talked to him?"

"I won't have much of a shot there. I'm not good with people, and tourists wouldn't like me."

Grams finished handing out pieces of cake and sat down opposite him. "You're a hard worker, and we'd vouch for you. There are plenty of jobs that wouldn't involve working with the lodge's guests."

"Maybe." His tone dripped doubt.

"I didn't think about insurance," Tessa said. "If you move out, your mother can't cover you on hers anymore, can she?"

He sniffed. "Hers ain't worth much anyway. But . . ."

When he paused, Grams leaned across the counter toward him. "Did you find out you have some kind of health problem? Are you okay?"

Luther exhaled a sigh. "Look. If I tell you something, you can't tell no one, understand? But I don't know what to do, and I don't know who to talk to."

Oh, crap. Secrets. Tessa hated hearing secrets. Then if she slipped up, everyone would know who told.

Grams had no such problem. "You've got us," she said.

He rubbed his forehead. "I got this girlfriend, see?"

Tessa blinked. This was not what she'd expected to hear.

"We love each other, and I'm gonna marry her, but I kinda . . . got her pregnant."

Grams licked her lips. "Even if you get insurance now, it won't pay for the baby. Companies won't cover preexisting conditions."

"I figured that, but the baby's gonna need lots of care, isn't it? Babies always need something. I have to find us a place and make more money."

Tessa's thoughts scrambled. She couldn't offer him insurance. She couldn't even offer him full-time work.

Grams raised an eyebrow at her. "You have an empty cabin, don't you?"

Not fair. Grams shouldn't have mentioned that without asking her first, but the more Tessa thought about it, the less it bothered her. What was she going to do with the small home? She looked at Luther. "The place was built for one person. It isn't very big, but you might like it there until you find somewhere else."

"But what if I find another job and can't work for you this summer?"

"You'll have to help out on Saturdays, and maybe your girlfriend could help us run the farm stand."

Luther lowered his head. He looked away from them. Had they insulted him? Hurt his feelings by acting like he couldn't handle things on his own? Tessa was about to apologize when he wiped at his eyes. Voice low, he said, "I'll make it up to you somehow. Honest, I will."

Grams' eyes misted. A knot formed in Tessa's throat. Embarrassed, she said, "Before you decide, what if I get the key and let you take a look at the place? It probably needs some work. I haven't been inside it for a few years now."

His cake forgotten, Luther pushed off his stool. He cleared his throat and gave a curt nod. Grams and Tessa grabbed their sweaters, and they headed to the bungalow to get the key. They found Ian on the front stoop, trying to peek in the window, to see if Tessa was home.

Tessa smacked her forehead. "I offered you an easy supper after Lily left, didn't I?"

"No, I offered to take you somewhere for standing you up, remember?"

Tessa shuffled her feet. "I need to show Luther the cabin before he leaves." She offered a quick introduction.

Ian grinned. "Good, I can go with you. I've been curious how it's laid out."

Tessa glanced at Luther, but he seemed all right with it, so she grabbed the key, and they crossed the side fields, planted with fruit trees and berry patches. The cabin sat back farther from the road, closer to the lake. Made of split logs, it had a rustic feel. The front stoop was small, but a screened-in deck opened off the kitchen in back. A one-car garage sat at the end of its driveway.

Tessa motioned toward the garage. "When we cleaned the cabin, we stored stuff in there. If this works, you should look through it."

She turned the key in the lock, and Luther's excitement got the better of him. He pushed the door open. He took a few steps inside the empty front room and his pale eyes gleamed. Dust coated the floors and surfaces, but he looked like he'd just won the lottery.

Grams smiled at him. "From that silly look on your face, I'm guessing you like the place?"

"You sure about this?" He looked out the back window at the lake. "It's like a dream. I like to fish, ya know." He stalked off to look at the two, small bedrooms separated by a bathroom. The farmhand had used the front room as an office. The kitchen, in back, was long and narrow with appliances and counter space on one end and an eating area on the other.

Ian studied the cabin with interest. "I've been thinking that some-day, I'd like to add separate cabins for guests to rent on one end of my lake property. This setup is pretty efficient."

"Gramps designed it." Tessa couldn't keep the pride out of her voice. "He was good at everything."

Grams nodded. "Tessa's right. The man wasn't too shabby when he wanted to get something done."

They all turned to look at Luther.

"What do you think?" Grams asked.

"When can we move in?"

"Whenever you get your stuff in order." Tessa looked at Ian. "Luther's going to live here and work for me on Saturdays for room and board."

"Just Saturdays? What about the rest of the week? Has he taken a new job?"

Luther went to stand beside Tessa. "I work for her during the summers."

"But he needs something permanent that's year-long." She gave Ian a meaningful look. "I can't offer him that."

"Are you saying he's up for grabs?" Ian narrowed his eyes, studying her.

"It looks that way."

"I can offer him full time, if you won't nail me to a wall for stealing him from you. I need someone to do lawn care at my place and clean stables, all the outside work. There'll still be plenty to do in winter—snow removal and upkeep."

Luther started his tap dance routine again. "I need decent insurance."

"I offer decent insurance and twelve dollars an hour, for starters."

Luther swallowed hard. He turned to Tessa. "Will you hate me?"

"You were a kid when I hired you. I knew you'd have to find something full time when you got out of high school."

Luther's expression went sullen. He glared at Ian. "Just so you know, the reason I need full-time work is my girlfriend's gonna have my baby. Does that change things between us?"

"I don't know. Will you still show up for work?"

Luther blinked, surprised by the question. "Well, yeah."

"Then what's the problem?"

Tessa watched them stare each other down and smiled. Ian recognized Luther's moodiness for what it was—a defense mechanism.

Luther broke first. "I just wanted you to know up front."

Ian nodded. "Duly noted. I appreciate honesty and hard work. We have a decent chance of getting along."

Luther jammed his hands in his jacket pockets. "I'm not good with people."

"Then stay away from them, but if they ask you something, be polite." Ian hesitated. "When can you start?"

Luther looked at Tessa.

"He's still in school," she said. "But he can probably work a few hours some evenings and full time once he graduates."

"I'll work long hours for you on Saturdays," Luther promised her.

"I wasn't worried about it, but I'll keep that in mind."

Luther looked around the cabin again and sighed. "I won't let my mom camp out here, I promise. She trashes whatever she has and invites her sleazy friends over. This will be for Kayla and me and our baby."

Tessa had never considered his mom using the cabin. She glanced at Grams. Luther's mom lived in a rundown house on a side street in town. Muscle cars and motorcycles were usually parked in its drive. She shook her head. "I don't want your mom's friends here."

Luther nodded. "Neither do I."

"Then we're fine. Take good care of it." Tessa pressed the key into his hand.

His eyes went wide. "Just like that? We can move in now?"

"You have to finish high school."

"We will. I promise." Then he shrugged his shoulders and tried to look cool.

Grams cleared her throat. "Well, now that everything's settled, I'm an old woman. I need to get home to watch my Saturday night British comedies."

No one would call Grams old. She had enough energy to drive most people into the dirt. Tessa laughed. "I forgot how much you love those."

"What's not to love? Gray-haired humor." Grams started out the door. Tessa and Ian followed her. Tessa told Luther, "Lock up when you leave."

He looked away from her again, and she didn't press it.

On the way to the farmhouse, Ian said, "Supper should be interesting tonight. I won't gloat that I got a new worker." At her sour look, he said, "I'll be good to him."

"You'd better be."

He laughed. "Or the next time I'm in a pickle . . ."

"I'll add vinegar." Tessa stayed to wave Grams away when they reached her SUV, and then she stopped to stare at a low, expensive sports car parked by her front door. "Whose is that?"

Ian beamed. "Lily helped me pick it out."

Tessa couldn't hide her surprise. "It's yours?"

"Bought it yesterday."

A Mustang. Mustard yellow. How practical was that? She didn't know what to say. How was he going to haul things? Carry heavy loads?

"You don't like it." He sounded disappointed.

What was wrong with her? She was ruining the fun of a new car. "I forgot you were going car shopping."

He opened the passenger door for her. "You don't lie very well."

She sighed. He was right. She usually said what was on her mind. After he settled behind the wheel, she tried again. "I've lived in the country too long. Gotten too practical. Don't pay any attention to me."

He glanced at her jeans. "You might want to run inside to change. I thought we'd try the seafood place in Columbus."

She pressed her lips together to keep from saying something stupid and climbed out of the car. By the time they drove to Columbus and back, it was going to be a late night. She usually called it quits early on Saturdays. She'd rather drive into town and hit the pizza place, but Ian was probably used to upscale restaurants.

He followed her inside the house and waited until she came out, wearing a knee-length, flowing, flowered skirt and a white, boat-necked blouse. "You look great."

No, she didn't. She'd worked all day, and her copper hair had gone frizzy in the bakery's humidity. Her long legs looked pale as paste in the winter months, and she hadn't bothered with any more than the basic makeup. But she kept her thoughts to herself.

The drive to the city took forty-five minutes, and she shook her head as Ian revved his car's engine every chance he got. She reminded herself that he hadn't owned a car in the city. Men liked their toys. If this made him happy, and he could afford it, why not? Once winter came, and the roads clogged with snow, he might have to buy a second vehicle.

It had been a long day—Tessa enjoyed watching the scenery stream past her and she relaxed as the miles flew by. When they reached the restaurant, Ian held her chair when the hostess led them to their table. He ordered wine and insisted on her choosing an appetizer. "You've been so nice to me, let me do this for you."

Oh, hell, why not? Tessa decided to flush her usual frugality and went with the flow. When she ordered fried calamari, Ian raised his eyebrows, surprised.

"I pictured you as a shrimp cocktail girl," he said.

"I am usually, but variety's nice once in a while." But not too often. Probably why she worked outside and baked in good weather and wrote during her months of hibernation. She'd have to cook Ian something out of the ordinary some night for supper, though. She'd been playing it safe with standard fare.

They talked about Luther over their entrees and changed to small talk and laughter over dessert.

"I bought one of your books and read it," Ian told her.

She stared. "I write romance."

"Yup, that's what it seemed like. Girl meets boy. Boy screws up. Boy works hard to win her back. Happy ending."

"Romances always have happy endings."

"In books." He smiled. "I like your writing style."

Her eyes danced with humor. "And the book?"

His grin could mesmerize. "Well, I'm guessing most guys don't make a habit of reading mushy stuff, but I'm glad I read yours."

"But one's enough?"

He laughed. "Probably, unless you put a lot more sex in the next one."

She shook her head. "I write *sweet* romances."

"Not a guy thing, we like action, in and out of bed."

"I'll remember that if I ever decide to change the audience I write for."

He reached across the table to lay his hand over hers. "No need for that. I like you just the way you are."

She couldn't finish her coffee. A lump lodged in her throat. Her heart felt like it enlarged. Could a compliment turn you into an idiot? She searched for words, didn't find many. "Thank you."

He pulled his hand away, embarrassed. "You're the best, Tess. Remember that."

By the time they started for home, Tessa realized that it had been a long time since she'd enjoyed herself so much.

When Ian parked by her front door, he asked, "Supper tomorrow?"

"Grams always comes to my place on Sundays."

"Good, I like her. See you at six?"

Couldn't the man order a pizza? But then she shrugged. Why not? It would make Grams' night. "See you then."

He gave a smile and tilted sideways. Was he going to kiss her goodnight? She stiffened. So did he.

"Let me help you with your door. I always reach over Lily. Sorry. It's habit." But he sounded as surprised with himself as Tessa was.

"I can open my own door, but thanks." She slid out faster than usual. "See you tomorrow."

Tires squealed as he lowered his foot on the gas. Tessa stared after him as he sped away. Okay, they'd had an awkward moment. Who didn't? Then she sighed. A mustard-colored Mustang. Lily was going to take to living in the country like oil takes to water.

Chapter 5

Tessa stayed in her pajamas on Sunday morning. She sprawled on her comfy couch and read the Sunday paper while she drank coffee and ate cinnamon rolls. No one came to visit on Sunday mornings, except for today. Someone knocked on the door at eleven.

Pulling on a robe, she cracked the door and frowned at Luther. "Is everything okay?"

Luther pushed the door wider to introduce her to Kayla. "I told her about you and the cabin. We're moving in today, if that's all right." He looked down at his feet. "And Kayla would like to start doing the summer gardening jobs I usually do."

Tessa stepped back to let them inside. "It's heavy work." The girl couldn't weigh more than a hundred and twenty pounds. Medium height and mousey, she looked like a sharp noise could give her heart failure. She had a washed-out look about her, as if life hadn't treated her kindly. Well, it hadn't, had it? Tessa knew the girl's family. They lived two towns over. Everyone knew the mother called for help when the domestic abuse got to be too much, but she never pressed charges.

"I'm stronger than I look." Kayla stood straighter. Tessa liked it that the girl stood up for herself, but she still doubted she could do the work Luther did. "Luther says you use a tractor to mow and garden. I can do that. And I like working outdoors. If it's something too heavy, Luther can help me on Saturdays."

Tessa knew Kayla was right. If Tessa shifted the workload, so that anything heavy or requiring handiwork got scheduled for Saturdays, Kayla could take over the gardening and help with the farm stand during the week. She shrugged, "Okay."

"Am I hired?" Kayla's body tightened like a spring.

"We'll give it a try." Tessa had no desire to hire high school kids she didn't know. They might very well be good, but there was always the start-up, learning curve. Luther could train Kayla.

Luther's shoulders relaxed. "The truth is, now we can afford to spend some of our savings to buy used furniture."

Tessa frowned, trying to remember. "Did you look in the cabin's garage? Grandpa had furniture made to fit the rooms in the house, but it's pretty rustic. If you don't want it, I'll have it stored upstairs in the barn."

"I forgot," Luther said. "I walked out to the lake and saw the short pier there, and I found fishing gear on the back deck. I got pretty stoked. There's furniture?"

"My grandpa made some out of logs. A kitchen table and benches. The frame for a couch, but the cushions were too old to save. A bed frame and some end tables."

Luther reached for Kayla's hand. "If those are still there, we could buy a new mattress."

Tessa waved them away. "Go check it out. The key's on the chain I gave you. I hope we saved it all." She shrugged. "There might even be a rowboat. George liked to fish." George had gotten sick a few months after Grandpa. Just like Gramps, George went to the hospital to die. He didn't have family to visit him or attend the funeral, just friends from town. Cleaning out his cabin was so depressing, Tessa and Grams had just lugged everything worth keeping to the garage, given anything of value to the Goodwill, and tossed everything else.

Luther could hardly stand still. He and Kayla said hurried goodbyes and took off. Tessa headed for the bathroom. She'd taken a shower and pulled on jeans and an old sweater when Luther knocked on her door again.

"Kayla says we should pay you for the furniture and boat. Can you take it out of her wages a little each week?"

"Nope, when George moved in there, it was furnished. It's not as furnished for you, but what's there came with the cabin. And that's the end of it." When Luther opened his lips to argue, Tessa said, "If Kayla doesn't like it, have her talk to me."

Luther's eyes went round. "No, never mind, thank you. We'll see you next Saturday."

"See you then."

He left with a bounce in his step.

Good. If Tessa had to deal with one more interruption today, she might hurt somebody. She hit the couch again to watch a movie she'd rented—*Hansel and Gretel: Witch Hunters.* She'd been looking forward to watching it for months, but had never gotten around to it. Today was the day. And boy, was it good!

The action and suspense energized her, so when it finished, she started making supper for Grams and Ian. She and Ian had seafood last night, but she'd bought fresh salmon when she went to the meat market. She made rice pilaf as a side dish with roasted asparagus and lemon meringue pie—one of Grams' favorites.

Grams got to the house first. When she walked in the kitchen, she gave a contented sigh. "It's like someone made all of my favorites just for me."

Tessa laughed. "It's possible I tried."

Grams glanced at the DVD case on the kitchen counter. "Really? Why not something fun and romantic? A chick flick?"

"Get real."

Fifteen minutes later, Ian pulled into the drive. It wasn't like him to be late, and when she welcomed him into the kitchen, his black mood preceded him.

"Is everything all right?" Tessa asked.

"No." Ian shoved a bottle of wine toward her. "Someone broke the padlock on my horse barn and sprayed graffiti on every single stall."

Grams and Tessa froze to stare at him. Nothing like that had ever happened in Mill Pond.

He let out a frustrated sigh. "I thought people might worry about a new resort on the lake, but I didn't think anyone would try to sabotage me."

Grams shook her head. "No one does things like that here."

"Really?" His voice dripped sarcasm. "I don't think the tooth fairy spray painted my stalls."

His tone surprised Tessa. He didn't need to talk to Grams like that. Her tone sharper than she intended, she said, "It's never happened before. People grumble or complain, but no one's stooped to property damage."

Ian ran a hand through his dark hair. "Sorry, I'm just annoyed. I'm working so hard to finish projects and open the place, something like this never occurred to me."

Grams and Tessa looked at each other. It hadn't occurred to them either.

"Can you fix it?" Tessa asked.

Ian nodded. "I talked to one of the contractors on the site. He said to use a special paint thinner, a power washer, and sandpaper. It's going to take me a few days to remove it, though. But I'll get it done. A little spray paint isn't going to slow me down."

Grams still seemed stunned. "Could this be personal? Is somebody mad at you about something?"

"Me?" Ian shook his head. "No one I can think of."

Tessa led them to the table. Witches had caused dark deeds in the movie. Someone was practicing dark deeds in Mill Pond. "We can talk about it over supper. Let's eat before everything's cold."

The vandalism had unsettled everyone. They ate and made small talk, but Tessa could tell each of them was thinking about what had happened.

When they finished the meal, Ian said, "You went to a lot of trouble, and I ruined our moods. I'm sorry."

"I'd be upset, too, if I were you," Tessa said. "No worries."

Grams left, fretting. Ian left, upset. And Tessa felt like she'd been hit with a stun gun. This was *so* not like Mill Pond; she couldn't wrap her mind around it.

Chapter 6

Tessa was working in her lean-to greenhouse on the back of the garage when a familiar red SUV pulled into her drive. *Darinda!* She hurried to greet her childhood friend.

Darinda crossed the yard to hug Tessa to her. A breeze tossed her short, black curls around her heart-shaped, cocoa-colored face. "Girl, I've missed you. I have today off, so thought I'd bug you a while."

It was a fact of life—a real bummer—that when Darinda had summers off from teaching, it was Tessa's busiest time in the gardens and farm stand. And when Tessa could be more flexible in the colder months, Darinda was teaching. They often teased that they were star-crossed, but somehow they always made time for each other.

Darinda's two, little boys raced to Tessa and each hugged a leg. "Do you have cookies?" Gianni, the five-year-old, asked.

"Chocolate chip?" Luigi, his three-year-old brother, specified.

Tessa hugged them both at the same time. "Hmm, we'll have to look in the cookie jar, won't we?"

The boys ran toward the house. Darinda and Tessa followed behind them. They were climbing on stools at her kitchen island when she pushed the cookie jar toward them. "Well?"

She always kept it stocked. The cookie jar, in her house, was never empty. "Well?"

Luigi's face fell as he pulled out a raisin-oatmeal.

"Try again."

A dimpled hand disappeared into the ceramic jar and came out with a chocolate chip cookie. A grin split his face.

Darinda's eyes narrowed. "Those weren't in your case this weekend."

"I always keep chocolate chips in the jar. They're every boy's favorite."

"You got that right. Even the big boys. Which reminds me ..." Darinda went to the refrigerator and poured four glasses of milk. Then she reached for a cookie, too. "I've heard you've been seeing a big boy lately. Are these cookies for him?"

"No, Ian's just a friend, a neighbor."

Gianni dug in the jar and laid out each kind of cookie he could find—sugar, oatmeal raisin, chocolate chip, and peanut butter.

"Whoa there!" Darinda waggled a finger. "Pick two. That's your limit, Bug Boy."

Tessa laughed. Gianni had taken a big interest in bugs lately. She'd bought him a cricket cage for his last birthday, and according to Darinda, it had housed all kinds of disgusting insects, even a toad or two.

Darinda tousled her son's hair. "We don't bake many cookies at our place, so they always look forward to coming here. Not just for the snacks. You're their favorite aunt."

Tessa wasn't really an aunt, but she and Darinda had been fast friends since Darinda's parents moved to Mill Pond and enrolled Darinda in Tessa's fourth grade class. At first, the other kids at school gave Darinda a hard time, but after she and Tessa became odd versions of the Bobbsey twins, they came around. Darinda was too funny for most people to resist. Her father was an ophthalmologist, and her mom was a professor of English at the local campus.

When Darinda graduated college as an elementary school teacher, she often joked that her parents should have known that rubbing shoulders with so many white people would lower her expectations. And then Darinda had met and married David Danza, an Italian who raised chickens, ducks, and geese. David loved all things food as much as Tessa did. Two kids later, he and Darinda seemed pretty darned happy together.

"How did you get off on a school day?" Tessa asked, running a critical eye over her friend. She didn't look sick. Neither did the boys. As a matter of fact, Darinda looked especially attractive today, but then, when didn't she? The girl knew how to dress.

"David had to meet with the new owner of Lakeview Stables. Ian wants David to be one of his suppliers. My parents are on a trip, so there wasn't anyone to watch the boys. I never take off days at school, but this was important to David, so ..."

"Good, you have some spare time to spend with me."

Darinda's dimple showed. "Boys, it's time for girl talk. Why don't you go outside and play on the tire swing?"

When Tessa was little, her grandpa had hung the swing in the old oak on the far side of the driveway, and he'd built her a tree house in some of the lower branches. The boys took off to have fun. When the door slammed behind them, Darinda's grin turned naughty. "Your big boy might be a friend and neighbor, but we've heard that you treat him very well."

Tessa snorted. "Who wouldn't? He's easy to get along with, so it's no big deal."

"When he talked to David on the phone, he said he'd invited you to his place tonight to show you all the improvements. He's going to grill for you, too."

That worried Tessa. Ian and a grill? But anyone could make hamburgers, right?

Darinda's dark eyes gleamed with curiosity. "I've heard he's a looker. Come on. Spill. Any sparks flying?"

"Yeah, between him and his fiancée." Tessa laughed at the disappointment on Darinda's face. "He's safe. That's why I'm comfortable around him."

Darinda heaved a dramatic sigh. "Damn, girl, you're no fun. I had high hopes for this one. But see here, you're spending time with him and you seem to be surviving just fine. It's time, friend. You're one fine woman. You've got to find yourself a man."

"Not all of us bump into a David." That was literally how Darinda met her husband—in a fender bender. Her fault, but no insurance cards exchanged hands. Instead, David said he'd consider his smashed fender as only a scratch if she'd go out to supper with him. The rest was history.

Darinda pursed her lips. "Well, I came over here to get all the scoop, and there isn't any."

"Did he tell you about his horse stalls?"

When Tessa finished her story, Darinda shook her head. "All the farmers David's talked to are happy Ian's opening a resort here. It'll only make things better. We have so many specialty farms in the area, it will bring in more business."

"Grams and I were shocked when he told us about it." Tessa cleared away the empty milk glasses and asked, "Wine?"

"Ooh, a little more temptation. Why not? One glass to celebrate friendship." When Tessa brought a bottle of rosé and two glasses,

Darinda nodded. "Perfect, something light." She poured some for herself and pushed the bottle to Tessa. "David's going to have a carry-in at our place to welcome Ian to the community. Put it on your calendar for Sunday, May nineteenth."

Tessa wrote it down. She knew better than to think she'd remember it without a note. "What do you want me to bring?"

"A dessert. David's making his famous brick chicken. I happen to love your tiramisu. Just saying."

Tessa grinned. "Okay, I got the hint. I'll bring it."

Darinda looked at the clock on the kitchen wall. She sighed. "I actually have stuff to do, so I guess I'd better get moving. I'll quit making plans for your wedding, but I'm not giving up hope. It's time you start looking around again." When Tessa didn't reply, Darinda put her hands on her hips. "Oh, be like that, but I'm right. Your libido can't be totally dead. That man should wake *something* up."

"He has. He's fun to cook for."

"Oh, pooh!" She stalked outside to collect her boys, and Tessa walked with her. She handed Gianni and Luigi each a baggie with a few cookies in it, and Darinda pulled her into another hug. "See you on the nineteenth."

Tessa waved them off, then went back to the greenhouse to clean up the mess she'd made potting the tomato plants. It was almost time to get ready to go to Ian's. On her way to the house, she noticed the daffodils were blooming in the beds that lined the picket fence. Early tulips added bright shades of red and orange. Ian needed to plant old-fashioned bushes and flowers around his lodge to make it look homier, maybe lilacs and spirea, hollyhocks, and rose bushes.

Her mind went to her conversation with Darinda. She hadn't really thought about having Ian stop in for supper most nights. It just seemed convenient for both of them. That way, neither of them had to eat alone. But she didn't like the idea of people talking about them. When she drove to his place, she meant to ask him about it, to see how he felt.

Her chance came while she stood on his back patio, watching him grill steaks. "My friend, Darinda, stopped by today. Seems the whole town is gossiping about how much time we spend together." She braced herself, ready for his reaction.

He laughed. "Everybody talks about everything. You're the one who told me this is a small town, that nothing's secret. But people are getting the idea. I'm engaged, and we're just friends. It might not work if you were—" He stumbled to a stop.

Tessa frowned. "If I were . . . what?"

He hesitated, obviously choosing his words carefully. "Everyone knows you don't want to meet anyone, that you've sworn to remain a spinster."

"A spinster?" Her spine stiffened. "Isn't that a little old-fashioned? Women who choose to stay single aren't spinsters anymore."

He fumbled to reword his reply. "People know you're not interested in men."

"That's not fair either. I like men. I just don't want to date or marry them."

He sighed. "I like you just the way you are."

Her brows furrowed in disgust. Those words had made her all gooey inside once. Not this time. "Lucky me."

He took the steaks off the grill and covered them with foil to let them rest. "I'm not giving you a steak knife tonight. You might stab me with it."

"Forks don't feel much better."

He laughed. "After we eat, I want to show you all the work that's been done. The place is beginning to shape up."

She shook off her aggravation and put it behind her. She was looking forward to his tour. "I heard you saw David Danza today, Darinda's husband."

"He's going to be one of my suppliers. Nice guy." Ian led her into the lodge's kitchen, and they settled at the small table near the window. He took baked potatoes out of the oven and shook a tossed salad out of a bag, into a bowl. "I went all out," he teased.

"How many suppliers have you lined up?" she asked.

They talked business while they ate. Ian had been busy. He'd talked to almost every specialty farmer in the area. "Thanks for cluing me in about them," he said. "Which brings me to you. I've talked to a baker one town over about supplying me with bread, so that's covered. Can I sign you up for pies and desserts?"

They crunched numbers and Tessa nodded. "That's doable. I can manage that."

Satisfied, Ian leaned back in his chair. "I'm hoping to open for business by the middle of June. Not everything will be done, but enough to do a test run and advertise for the Fourth of July."

A mother duck with a row of ducklings paddled along the shore toward his pier.

"She comes every day," Ian said. "She must like that spot."

Tessa shook her head. "Sam used to feed her. He always had scraps of bread to toss to her."

"I have bread." Ian went to take a few slices out of the loaf he'd bought.

Tessa led him to the end of the pier, tore her slice of bread into small pieces, and tossed them into the water. The ducks scrambled for them. A broad smile on his face, Ian did the same.

"If you do that every evening when she comes, you'll have a regular," Tessa said.

"I'd like that."

They wandered back toward the house, stopping to look at the shade plants that circled the tall trees in the yard.

"The beds are a mess," Tessa said, "but Luther knows what a weed is and what isn't. He's worked with hostas and bleeding hearts. He can clean these up in no time."

"You've trained him well for landscaping, haven't you?"

"He's a fast learner. Just treat him with respect. If he likes you, he'll work his ass off. If he doesn't, you're doomed."

"I'll remember that."

Once back in the kitchen, Tessa helped clear the dirty dishes off the table, rinse them, and load them in the dishwasher. "Thanks for the supper. It was great."

"We can eat dessert on the back patio after I show you around."

"You made dessert?"

"Three flavors of ice cream to choose from with the best jar toppings in the store."

Tessa laughed. She didn't care. She didn't have to cook. Ian motioned her toward the door. "The grand tour."

The ground had been leveled for the tennis courts between the house and the lake. "They should be done by the end of next week." He showed her the work he'd done inside the horse barn. Half of the graffiti was cleaned off. Tessa stared at what was left. Go Away scrolled across one stall. City Folks Belong In The City said another.

She shook her head. "This graffiti's almost too nice."

"New York kids would make this stuff look tame, but boy, there was a lot of it. A pain to clean. David thinks someone just wants me to leave." He spread his hands in confusion. "But why? Most people like the idea of a resort."

"Kids would just paint something crude on the outside."

"Unless they didn't want to be seen. I've gone over and over it in my mind. None of it makes sense." Ian turned to leave. "We're having a nice night. Let me show you the golf course."

Big machines sat on his side field and stakes marked where each green should go.

"Do you play golf?" he asked.

"Used to. I'm pretty good at it." Her mom practically lived at the country club in the summers. She'd signed Tessa up with every pro around.

He beamed. "We'll have to have a friendly match sometime."

She doubted that. He seemed pretty competitive, and she hated to lose. Their game should be interesting.

"Come see the great room. We've redone that, too."

A blue heron flew overhead as they crossed the front yard to the house. Tessa wondered if it was the one she'd nicknamed Bill that spent most mornings on the edge of her shoreline.

When she stepped through the lodge's front double doors, she sucked in her breath. Three brown leather sofas formed a seating area in front of the tall, fieldstone fireplace. Dark-green leather recliners were scattered in small groupings around the rest of the room. A counter with a granite top stood ready to check in guests. The only jarring elements were two huge crystal chandeliers that hung from the ceiling, but they didn't detract too much from the rustic charm of the room.

Ian followed her gaze. "The chandeliers don't quite fit the mood, but Lily saw them online and liked them."

Tessa tried to be diplomatic. "They're beautiful." *For castles or ballrooms.* But she didn't add that.

He grinned, clearly hearing what she didn't say. "As you see, no tables, no rugs. You promised to help me search out antiques," he reminded her.

"When do you want to go?"

He looked sheepish. "Tomorrow or Wednesday, and can you drive? My car doesn't have much of a trunk."

She didn't say it. She thought it, but clamped her lips shut. Instead, she nodded. "I have both days open. What would work better for you?"

"Wednesday. The pod with my stuff from New York is coming tomorrow morning and then I have to drive into the city to talk to my banker. I can switch, though, if I need to."

She shook her head. "Wednesday's fine. I'll drag you to all the small antique shops around here. There are a few in every town."

They went out to the back patio and sank into the Adirondack chairs to eat their sundaes and watch the sun go down. Ian reached for her hand, stopped, and pulled back. He'd been *that* close. Tessa could almost feel his fingers twine through her own. She sighed. How would that feel? Wanted? Cherished?

"Lily would love this." His voice was brusque. "She loves water. Her favorite vacation spots are islands."

Time to reel it in. Tessa swept the fantasies out of her head, made herself concentrate on the moment. "Like the Caribbean or Hawaii?"

Ian nodded. "She travels a lot with her job. Goes all over the world to work with clients. Everywhere she goes, she has fun. She says she's ready for somewhere to relax that she can use as a home base."

"And she chose here?" Tessa loved the Midwest, but she didn't see Lily embracing the slower pace, the abundance of green.

Ian frowned. "It wouldn't be her first choice, but I couldn't afford a resort on one of the coasts, so we decided I'd start here. When this makes a profit, then we can add another one."

"And Lily's all right with that?"

"Why wouldn't she be? It's good business sense. Lily understands business."

If he said so. Tessa would never have guessed it. The sun was low enough to tint the bottom of the clouds a coral pink. She stretched and yawned. Parts of her body she'd thought were dormant suddenly tingled. *Time to get out of here.* "This has been fun, but I want to get home before dark. Good luck with your banking tomorrow."

He seemed distracted, but gave a curt nod. "See you on Wednesday. Are we getting an early start?"

"Might as well. What if I pick you up at eight?"

He smiled. "Office hours, eight to five. I'm used to those."

She smiled, too, and when he started to stand to walk her to her pickup, she waved him off. She didn't want to brush up against him. Hell, she didn't even want to be close to him right now. "Enjoy the sunset. And thanks for supper."

"I owed you."

A splash of cold water. Those words didn't warm the cockles of her heart. On the drive home, she brooded. When Ian had reached for her hand, she'd *wanted* him to take it. Not good. They were just friends. Period. Nothing more.

Maybe they needed to spend less time together. This was the second time Ian had reached for her and then blabbed away about Lily to make it clear to Tessa that it had been a mistake. Her frown deepened. What would she have done if he *had* taken her hand? *Crap.* A surge of emotion that had been bottled up inside her for too long welled to the surface. Would she have crawled over the arm of his chair and attacked him?

It wouldn't have happened. She'd have pulled away first. Right?

Chapter 7

A blue jay woke her on Tuesday morning. The damned bird sat in the old oak and called incessantly until she gave up and got out of bed. She looked out the window and saw a hawk sitting on the white picket fence. The blue jay blasted his warning to everyone else. *Danger! Beware!*

She padded to the kitchen, flipped on the coffee pot, and went to the front door to fetch the morning paper. Mill Pond didn't bustle with news, but she liked to keep up. Grandma's church was doing an ice cream social on Sunday. She went to write that on the calendar in her kitchen. If she missed being there, Grams would string her up by her thumbs. Or worse.

She wouldn't see Ian today, and twenty-four hours stretched before her. She decided to work in her gardens, get everything caught up, and have an omelette for supper tonight—simple and easy. She started at her compost piles on the side of the garage, where she faithfully tossed scraps, grass clippings, and coffee grounds in the chicken wire structures. She'd filled three wheelbarrows with the contents from one and was putting more mulch around the strawberry plants in the third bed when a car pulled into her drive. She glanced up and frowned at the unfamiliar vehicle.

Then the door opened and Gary stepped out. She froze. Her heart stopped. Was that possible? Could she die from shock or surprise? Maybe if she didn't move, sat absolutely still like a rabbit, he wouldn't notice her. No such luck. He looked her way and started toward her. She put up a hand to stop him. "No, don't come any closer. Just get back in your car and leave."

Sunlight glinted off his light-blond hair. His sky-blue eyes narrowed on her. He could be an Adonis, but Greek gods were shifty, too, weren't they? "We need to talk."

"No, we don't. We have nothing to say to each other. Go away."

He planted his feet and didn't move. He wore the same jean jacket he'd worn in college. No, it couldn't be, but it sure looked the same. His worn jeans hugged his long legs. Too good-looking. She should have known. Good-looking men couldn't be trusted.

He tucked his sunglasses in his jacket pocket. "I know I hurt you. I didn't mean to. It's time we moved on."

"We have moved on. You're married. You're happy. Leave me alone."

"Tessie . . ."

"Don't call me that."

"What should I call you?"

"From a long distance. Leave a message on my machine."

He jutted his jaw forward. He was as tall as Ian, but not as muscular. He took a step closer. "I'm not leaving until we talk."

"Then your wife's never going to see you again. How sad." Tessa pushed to her feet. She wiped her hands on her jeans and started toward the kitchen door. "Don't follow me. You're not invited in."

He didn't listen. He made up the distance between them more quickly than she thought he could. She opened the door, slid inside, and started to close it. He put his foot between the door and the doorframe.

"I have a butcher knife. If you want to keep your toes, get them off my property."

He pushed, and she scooted across the oak floorboards. Then he stepped inside and closed the door behind him. He leaned against it. "I still care about you. That's why I came. "

"It took you a while. I'm over it. I'm fine. If you feel better now, you can leave."

He smiled. "Sadie's pregnant."

She turned her back on him and hung her ratty jacket on the peg by the door. She stepped out of her shoes and padded into the kitchen.

"My parents talked to a few people about you and it sounds like your life just stopped; you've never dated anyone else, and you don't intend to. That's just wrong."

"You have no right to lecture me about what's wrong or right."

He flinched. "I'm happy. I want you to be happy."

"I am. I like my life."

He raised a blond eyebrow. He'd always called her out when she spouted bullshit.

"I've never liked anyone more in my life than I like you."

Oh, brother. She should have worn boots. She was going to be wading through a lot of crap soon. "I'm thrilled," she said. "You've made me feel all warm and fuzzy. You've done your duty. See?" Her lips curled in a fake smile. "There. Feel better? This isn't about me. It's about you. You were a turd and it's not your usual style. But you were never a knight in shining armor, either, and I don't need to be rescued. So leave."

He went to the coffee pot, poured himself a cup, and went to reheat it in the microwave. They'd always been comfortable with each other. But things had changed. She scowled.

He took his mug to the kitchen table and pulled out a chair. He stretched his long legs and cocked his head toward her. "I came to talk."

She sighed. Gary came across as easy-mannered, and for the most part, he was. But when he made up his mind about something, nothing could shake him. She sat across the table from him and glared.

"I didn't want to fall in love with Sadie," he said. "I thought I was completely happy with you."

She grimaced. "This is supposed to make me feel better?"

"I want to explain."

She felt like sticking her fingers in her ears, like small children do, but he'd just outwait her. So she crossed her arms. The sooner he spilled his guts, the sooner she could get on with her life.

"I cared about you. Still do." He leaned forward to make his point. "I hate it that I blew it, that I hurt you. And I've gone over and over what I did, what happened. The only thing I can say is that I was crazy about you as a friend, but with Sadie, there was chemistry. The *like* was there, but so was the desire."

Her hand went to her throat. It was true. She wasn't the type who could stir passion in a man. They might like her, admire her, care about her, but they wouldn't *love* her. Hurt clogged her throat. She couldn't talk. She blinked and looked away. What could she say? "Why didn't you love me?" She'd thought he had.

He frowned. He read her too well. "I loved every minute I spent with you. You know that, right?"

Voice small, she said, "But I wasn't enough. I'm never enough."

Eyes wide, he stared. "My God, is that what you think? Who knows how that works? I sure as hell don't, but you've got it wrong. Some man's going to look at you and want you more than he's ever wanted anything in his life."

She released a sigh of disgust. "Isn't that what every boyfriend says to the girlfriend he's just jilted?"

"But it's true." Gary ran both hands through his wavy, blond hair, mussing it—which only made him look better. "You only need to let it happen, Tessa, and it will. You're too wonderful to live alone."

She pushed away from the table and walked to the door. She opened it and motioned for him to leave. "You've had your say. I listened to you. Have a nice life and congratulations on the baby."

He slowly rose, carried his cup to the sink, and rinsed it. He stopped and bent close to her on his way out. "Let love in, Tessie. It will find you."

She nodded for him to leave.

Once he drove away, she closed the door and slumped against it. She shut her eyes and pushed her feelings into their usual hiding place. She didn't want to deal with them.

Tessa couldn't settle enough to concentrate on anything for the rest of the afternoon, so she finally gave up, got in her pickup, and drove into town to have supper. Maybe the bustle and noise of Mill Pond's favorite diner would quiet her thoughts. She sat at a small table for two and ordered the high-calorie meal that she usually avoided—pork Manhattan with stuffing arranged between a slice of white bread cut in half, buried under lots of gravy. She was sipping her lemonade when Leona Jackson carried her Cobb salad over to join her.

Tessa wasn't in the mood for Leona, but she didn't want to be churlish. Subtleties rolled off Leona like water off a duck. Only rudeness slowed her down, and it took more than that to be rid of her. Tessa sighed and decided the planets had destined her day to be shitty.

Leona dropped into the chair across from her and smiled. Crocodile grins looked friendlier. The woman wanted something. She got right to it. "I met that nice neighbor of yours a few days ago, and my, oh my, is he handsome."

"He's nice, too. His fiancée has no idea how lucky she is." Tessa waited, but Leona managed not to hear the hint.

"That boy hardly ever comes to town. I hear he spends all of his free time with you." Leona narrowed her eyes, studying her, then shrugged. "Where's his girlfriend? Why isn't she with him?"

The waitress brought Tessa's food and refilled her lemonade. Once she left, Tessa looked at Leona. "Ian came early to get the lodge in shape as a resort. Once he gets things ready, Lily's going to move in with him."

If Leona knew the plan, soon the town would. Everyone would hear that Ian was engaged, and his fiancé would move in with him soon.

Leona pouted. "I wonder how long that will take. Passions can cool, can't they?"

Tessa chose not to respond. If anyone knew the answer to that, Leona would.

Leona sighed. "I mean, look at him—a total hottie. I bet he's used to getting plenty of female attention."

Tessa rolled her eyes. Was Leona declaring Ian fair game? She forced a smile and tried to change the topic. "Are you going to the church social on Sunday?"

Leona's expression lit up. "Why? Is your neighbor going to be there?"

Oh, boy, Ian might as well have a big target sign painted on his forehead. "I don't know. I haven't asked him."

Leona's enthusiasm faded. "But he might be?"

Tessa shrugged. "It's according to whether Lily's spending a long or short weekend."

Leona's ardor faded. "You're telling me he's well-and-truly taken."

"Pretty much."

Leona sighed. She finished her salad, and Tessa quit picking at her food. They paid their bills and Tessa drove home—her plan to boost her mood, a bust.

There was only one thing to do. She filled a coffee cup with dark cherry sorbet and reached for Ilona Andrews' latest urban fantasy. A few hours later, Kate Daniels and Curran had kicked every supernatural's butt. The book finished, Tessa felt better. She headed to bed.

Tomorrow morning, she'd pick up Ian and take him shopping for antiques. Appropriate because at the moment, she felt worn and weathered.

Chapter 8

Ian turned to give her a quizzical look. "You're awfully quiet this morning."

"I'm talked out."

"Really?" He frowned at a pasture, filled with alpacas. "People don't raise and eat those, do they?"

Tessa smiled. "That's Bob Thorton's farm. His wife, Ester, dyes and weaves the wool."

"Into what?"

"All sorts of things, but mostly wall hangings. She sells them online."

Ian shook his head. "You know, before I moved here, I thought the Midwest was pretty behind, out of the loop. I pictured farms and industry. But there's a lot more."

She rolled her eyes. "You're from New York, right?"

He nodded.

"In the Midwest, we think both coasts are too full of themselves."

He threw back his head and laughed. "I guess I deserved that. I talk about Indiana like it's behind the times."

She glanced his way. "So, what did you do in New York? What in the world brought you to Mill Pond?"

"Both fair questions." He hesitated. "I was a stock broker, made lots of money with my own investments. I worked for my brother in the summers when I was going through college. Construction." At her look, he grinned. "Lots of cement and earth moving. No flat tire changing. And once a year, our family all heads to a house on the beach in North Carolina. I have great memories from there. So I decided I wanted to open a resort."

"And you have the business know-how to make it work."

He nodded. "I've got all the big things covered. It's the small, everyday things that threw me a little, but I'm learning."

"Everyone wants you to succeed. If you have a problem, all you have to do is ask someone."

"I'm getting the feel of it. You guys do community really well."

"Better than I expected. Small towns don't welcome newcomers all that well. You've managed a small miracle. People are claiming you as one of our own."

"That's not typical?"

"Nope. Most people are born and raised here, so are their parents, and their parents' parents."

"So I'm lucky?"

She smiled at him. "I'd say you made your own luck."

"Thanks!" He looked at her. "Having you take me under your wing helped."

"We're . . ."

He grinned. "Neighbors. I know. Where are we going today?"

"I thought we'd start at an antique shop on the highway. It's my favorite, and then we can stop in Pierceton and Angola. If we come up empty, we'll take the round-about way home."

He grinned. "This sure is pretty country."

"I like it." She motioned toward a field with horses. "You have someone who knows horses to help you choose ones for your stables, right?"

His dark brows furrowed together. "I thought I'd buy one of each color." When her jaw dropped in shock, he laughed at her. "I bet on horse races. I know there are good horses and not so good horses."

She nodded, satisfied.

When she turned silent again, he frowned. "What's up? Something's bothering you."

"My ex came to visit me yesterday. Said he wants me to be happy. He and Sadie are expecting their first baby."

He gave a low whistle. "He's the guy who turned you off men, right?"

"Yup, that would be Gary."

He stretched his arm across the back of the seat to lay a hand on her shoulder. "Look, we're friends. If you ever need an ear, a shoulder to cry on, whatever, I'm here for you. It goes both ways. When you need something, let me know."

She gave a quick nod, and he pulled his hand away. "Hmm, no touching. Just like a cat." He gave her a stern look. "You know how to give, Tessa Lawrence, but you're not so good at receiving. You need to work on that."

Her shoulders stiffened. Her fingers gripped the steering wheel. "I've had enough lectures lately." Her voice sounded surly, even to her own ears.

"Okay, okay, I'll drop it. If you ever want to talk about it, though, I'm here." When she pulled into the gravel lot of the shop, he turned his attention to the rusted wash tub by the front door. A butter churn sat next to it. He gave her a questioning look. "You're sure this is a good place?"

"Shopping for antiques is a crap shoot. Sometimes, you get lucky. Sometimes, you find junk, but I like this place. Come on."

He followed her inside and stopped, surprised. "It's bigger than it looks."

The large pieces of furniture sat in the center, near the front of the store. Ian saw a long, trestle table and went straight to it. "I like this."

"Where would you put it?"

"Behind one of the leather couches. I could put a lamp and some memorabilia on it."

Tessa nodded. She could picture that. It would work.

He looked at the price. "Not cheap, but not terrible, either."

Tessa motioned to one of the clerks. "We're interested in this." They began haggling about prices. Ian watched, bemused. When they settled on a number, the woman behind the counter grabbed a Sold sticker. Tessa led Ian up and down aisles. They found two, matching side tables. He chose a big, wooden chest to use as a coffee table. "Can I stain it a different color?"

"Grams likes to refinish old furniture. She can help you."

He found some pink glass Depression-era dishes he liked. "We could put those in the corner cupboard over there."

By the time they paid for everything and loaded it into the back of her pickup, Tessa didn't think they could haul anything else that was very big.

"We can go to the small towns to look for little stuff, though, right?" Ian had the gleam in his eyes that true shoppers get. Tessa sighed. She avoided shopping as much as possible. It showed. Her outfits needed updating. She never thought about it until she stood next to Lily or Leona, but she could use some spiffing up. But today was dedicated to finding antiques for Ian's lodge, so she started toward Pierceton.

They hit every shop there and still went on to Angola. Ian bought an old-fashioned horse collar to hang on the wall. He bought a quilt. Tessa had to curb him when he found braided rugs in all sizes. They settled on a half dozen. By the time they started back to his lodge, she couldn't fit one more item in her truck.

Halfway home, Ian pointed at a root beer stand on the side of the road. "We should stop there, get something to eat. Then we don't have to worry about anyone taking what we bought."

Like he'd worried before. *Not.* She couldn't keep him out of a store. Tessa pulled in, and Ian pressed the button on the speaker to place their orders. Tessa got two chili dogs, and he got a pork tenderloin sandwich. When he bit into it, he groaned with pleasure. "I've heard about these. I've never had one."

"You've never had a PT deluxe?"

He shook his head. "I think it's a Midwest thing."

Tessa couldn't imagine life without those giant breaded treats. While they ate, they talked about where he was going to place each piece of furniture and each accessory he'd bought. On the drive back to his lodge, he could hardly wait to start carrying things inside.

Tessa hurried after him as he strode into the great room and smacked into him when he came to an abrupt halt. She peeked around him and gasped.

One of the two, huge, crystal chandeliers had smashed to the floor. Glass shards had sprayed everywhere.

Ian looked up and motioned to where it was mounted to the ceiling. It had obviously pulled away. "The same crew that installed my shower doors put up the chandeliers."

Enough said. Tessa took in the volume of the mess. "This is going to take hours to clean."

Ian's muscles bunched and his fingers curled into fists. "They're going to pay for the chandelier. I'll make sure of that, but Lily found these online. There were only two of them." He ran a hand through his dark hair. "I'm going to have to replace them both. One chandelier isn't going to work."

"Where did you find the workers you hired?" This crew must have put in as little effort as possible. Both projects they did were failures. "Ask around before you hire someone for your next job. People here will give you the names of people we trust." She pulled her cell phone out of her pocket and called Grams. "Ian's chandelier fell. He has a king-sized mess. We could use some help cleaning it up."

"I'll be there."

Ian shook his head. "You've already spent all day shopping with me. I can't ask you to help with this."

"You didn't, so quit wasting time. Find us some brooms."

He opened his mouth to argue, saw her expression, and headed to do as told.

A half hour later, Tessa stopped sweeping glass as cars started pulling into the drive. Ian dumped the pile they'd collected into a large trash can and looked up as David and Darinda hurried inside and stopped to stare.

"If I knew who screwed up both of your jobs, I'd kick their friggin' asses!" Darinda fumed.

David put a hand on her shoulder. He shook his head. "Nope, what's done is done, but it won't happen again. We'll recommend the right people for Ian."

Luther and Kayla knocked and stepped inside next. Luther stared. "Holy shit! What happened?"

Tessa pointed to the bare wires on the ceiling where the weight of the chandelier had broken away. "Shoddy workmanship. They didn't attach it right."

Kayla squared her shoulders. "Where are more brooms? Your cleaning supplies?"

Garth stepped through the doors next. "Lord almighty! I've never seen a mess like this."

Leona followed him into the room. Poured into a skintight dress and wearing high heels, she didn't look the part of clean-up help. Her streaked-blonde hair was pulled up in a sexy, mussy, Gibson-girl look. She went straight to Ian and pressed herself against his side. "Oh, darling, I bet you're upset. I'd do anything I can to help you."

Garth sniggered. "In that dress and shoes? You'll be lucky if you can keep your balance in here. Glass is everywhere. I want to see you bend over to sweep it up."

Leona glared at him. "What do you know? You play in grease all day."

"I sure as hell do. I can make your engine purr any time."

Her full, red lips opened in surprise. She pointed a finger at him.

"Watch your mouth, Garth Roarke, or I'll walk a picket line at your garage."

He grinned. "If you wear that dress, I'll bring you out bon-bons to keep your energy up."

Leona's comment was cut off when Grams strode into the room. She let out a long sigh. "This isn't right. No one's this lazy or stupid in Mill Pond. I'd demand my money back."

Ian shrugged. He'd gotten over his first burst of anger and looked around in awe. "I can't believe all of you came to help me."

Grams shook her head. "We couldn't leave you to clean up this mess alone. You don't deserve it."

While they worked, Evan Meyers—who owned the goat farm next to Tessa's property—and his wife came to help. Soon, other people from Mill Pond joined in. In a couple of hours, they were finished and people offered Ian sympathy and support. By the time everyone left, they'd carried all of the furniture from Tessa's pickup into the lodge and helped Ian find the right places for it.

Before people wandered off, Garth announced—loud enough for everyone to hear and spread the word—"I'm glad it wasn't vandalism this time, but you need to think about protecting your property, friend. If I were you, I'd pay for a security system. I have one for my garage."

Evan nodded. "You'll want one when you have guests start staying here. People like the idea of security."

Ian blinked, surprised. "I didn't think about it, but you're right. I have too much money invested here to not protect it."

"Smart man." Garth patted him on the back. "The sooner, the better. And call me before you have someone put up your next chandelier." He put out a hand to Leona. "Want me to walk you to your car, hon?"

"Hon!" She glared. "I've walked in heels this high since I was sixteen. I think I can manage."

"I'll pay if you'd like to go to Chase's Bar and have a drink to cool off with me."

Her eyes lit up. "I love his bar fries."

"You can order anything your little heart desires." Garth offered his elbow.

Leona latched on to it, and they left.

Everyone followed.

Alone with Tessa once more, Ian looked around the room. "It looks great, except for the missing chandelier."

She nodded. "Everything fits. It works." She glanced up at the empty ceiling. "Do you remember the black, iron chandeliers with the deer antlers we saw in Pierceton? I think they'd work here, and they were on sale."

His lips pressed into a firm line. "They'll probably work better, but Lily liked the crystal ones. She's going to be pretty disappointed when I tell her what happened."

Lily. Tessa swallowed . . . what? Bitterness? Disappointment? Then she mentally slapped herself. What was wrong with her? Lily was Ian's fiancée. Her vote should count more than anyone else's.

Tessa made a point of looking at her watch. "It's later than I expected. I bake with Grams all day on Thursdays. What if I order pizza for supper tonight? Does that sound all right?"

"I'll order it. You spent all day with me and then helped with clean-up when we got back. You deserve a break." He pulled out his cell phone and called the number she told him.

When the pizza came, they ate on Ian's back patio. He drank beer and she drank wine, and they tossed the cardboard box in the trash to clean up.

Before she drove home, she said, "You know, Garth's idea of a security system isn't half bad."

He nodded. "I'll call and get something set up tomorrow. My first thought when I saw the chandelier was that someone had broken in, too. Might as well do something about that."

"Are you coming for supper?" Tessa asked.

"Do you want me? I cost you a lot of time today."

"Thursdays are crock-pot days. Either that or peanut butter and jelly."

"I like grape."

He looked so distraught, she gave him a hug. "Hang in there, friend."

When he hugged her back, he held her a little longer than comfortable. All sorts of lust-filled zings zipped through her. The man felt good. She wanted to wrap her legs around his waist and jam her tongue down his throat. Not neighborly thoughts. His chest and abs felt rockhard. So were his thighs. So was . . . *oh, lord* . . . that again. She tried not to think about it. When he released her, he grinned. "And I don't like crunchy. I like smooth."

"What?" She looked at him, dazed.

"Peanut butter," he said.

She laughed, relieved they'd returned to safe ground. "My favorite, too. Got it."

On the drive back to her white bungalow, she tried to collect her thoughts. Oh, lord, her inner self was a slut. She'd have to keep that part of herself on a leash. *Down, girl, he's only a neighbor.*

Then her thoughts turned to the shattered chandelier on Ian's floor and the friends who'd come to help him. Mill Pond had embraced Ian as one of their own. But then, why wouldn't they? Ian was special.

Chapter 9

Grams stepped through the back door of the barn, into the kitchen, and shook her head at Tessa. "Your cute, little neighbor has had a rough time of it."

Tessa nodded. "It was nice of you to call in the cavalry to help him out."

"People wanted to come. We like that boy." Grams hung her sweater on a peg by the door and came to grab a stack of pie tins. "What are we making this week?"

Tessa nodded toward the bags of frozen peaches she'd taken out of her chest freezer. "Peach pies, sugar cream pies, and German chocolate pies."

"We'd better make extra German chocolates. Those are a thank-you to Garth, aren't they? He loves those."

Tessa smiled. "He loves anything with coconut in it."

"Coconut pie's easier." Grams started measuring flour into a large bowl.

"Too much like sugar cream." Tessa started putting the ingredients for rum cake de Maison on her side of the granite counter, including the fresh oranges and white rum.

"What kinds of cookies are we baking today?" Grams cut ice-cold butter into squares to add to the dry ingredients for the piecrusts.

"M&Ms, molasses, and sugar cookies." A little bit of everything.

Grams nodded, and she and Tessa got to work. They each had a routine, and they sailed through the morning.

Once the pies were in the oven, Grams said, "Rumor is Garth and Leona went back to his place after they left the bar last night."

"Really?" Tessa slid the last round cake pan into the bottom oven. "I'd have never pictured those two together." Garth was in his mid-thirties, a little shorter than Leona, with a belly that wasn't getting smaller. He wasn't bad looking, but he wasn't good looking either.

"He owns his own business, has a decent house with enough room for a hair salon downstairs, and he's financially stable," Grams said. "He's never been married, doesn't have kids, and Leona's car is on the fritz."

Tessa blinked. "Gee, put that way . . ."

Grams chuckled. "It just might work. What about you? I heard you had a visitor this week."

Tessa recounted the story about Gary stopping in and giving her a hard time about staying single.

"He's right," Grams said. "You're playing it too safe. It's time to live again."

Tessa frowned, tired of the lecture. "Maybe I'll drive into the city and stop at a bar, find someone fun."

Grams didn't take the bait. "Works for me. Just use protection."

"Yeah, right." Grams would have heart failure if Tessa actually picked up a stranger for a one-night stand.

Grams' expression softened. "So Gary's going to have a baby?"

"Don't go there."

"It's been a while since I've held a baby. I don't think that brother of yours is ever going to have one."

Craig was eight years older than she. He and his lawyer wife worked hard and played hard. "Craig and Nora would rather hit hot vacation spots and travel. Kids aren't on the agenda."

"Exactly. You're my only hope."

"Bull pucky." Tessa heated a double boiler to start her chocolate frosting.

"You can borrow anybody's kids in town that you want to. Everyone loves you. Even with background music, I won't buy your poor me routine."

Grams laughed. "Hey, an old lady has to try."

"Good effort, now move on."

They finished filling the long, glass dessert cases earlier than usual, and Grams gave her a merry wave as she sped to town to meet a friend. Tessa spent another hour filling shelves with condiments and getting the shop ready for business tomorrow, then wandered to the house.

Ian was coming for supper. And no, she wouldn't serve peanut butter and jelly. This morning, she'd started a turkey breast in the slow cooker to make French dip turkey sandwiches. She'd brought four of each cookie home for dessert and got busy making a Waldorf salad. When Ian walked through the back door and looked at the table, a grin crinkled his face.

"How do you do it?" he asked. "I'm starving. I made myself a grilled cheese for lunch, and it didn't fill me up."

She'd watched the man eat, and she couldn't believe he didn't weigh a thousand pounds. "How do you stay in shape?" she asked. "How do you have so many muscles?"

His grin widened, and he flexed his arm to show off his biceps. "You've noticed? I work out. I have a weight bench in my office, a chin-up bar, and I do a hundred push-ups at a time."

So that was the trick.

"I like to play sports, too. I haven't had the time lately, but I try to keep active."

She shook her head. "Well, you look good."

"You'd know." His chocolate-brown eyes sparkled. "You saw me in the shower."

She couldn't stop the blush that colored her cheeks. "I haven't told anyone about that."

"Lily's told everyone she knows. She thought it was hilarious."

Lily would.

"It makes for a great story." Tessa removed the skin from the turkey breast, sliced the white meat, and returned it to the sauce. A distraction. She didn't want to think about Ian pressed against the glass shower doors. She nodded to the crusty buns she'd toasted. "Let's eat."

When they sat at the table, Tessa asked, "Did you tell Lily about the barn stalls and the chandeliers?"

He nodded. "At first, she accused me of smashing them. She knew I didn't like them that much."

"And then?"

"Lily doesn't understand. She said that if Mill Pond doesn't want me and it's too hard to get started here, I should put a FOR SALE sign in front of the property and go back to finances."

Tessa stared. "Would you do that?"

"Hell, no." His voice turned steely. "If anything, the vandalism and mess-ups make me want to dig in more. Lily walks away from battles. I don't."

No, Ian wasn't the type to give up, she could tell.

They made it an early night. Friday would be a busy day for both of them. Tessa and Grams would work in the bakery all day tomorrow and Saturday. Lily was coming to town late Friday afternoon. Ian needed to conserve his strength. Tessa thumped her pillow when she fell into bed that night and drifted to sleep in an off mood.

Chapter 10

The phone rang at three in the morning.

Tessa grabbed it. "Grams?" Was she all right? Had she fallen? Had something happened?

A male voice answered. "Tessa, I'm in a bit of a jam."

Really? Tessa had to work in the bakery all day Friday and Saturday. "This had better be good."

"There's a bat flying around in my bedroom," Ian said. "A big one. How do I get rid of it?"

She groaned. "Do you have a tennis racket?"

"Somewhere. It's in a stack of boxes in the garage, not sure which one."

"Have you tried throwing dead bugs in the air and leading it outside?"

"You're not all that funny."

She sighed. "I'll be there in a few minutes."

She put a bra on under her pajama top, decided her pj bottoms were good enough, and grabbed her own racket. On the drive to Ian's, she rolled down the window of her pickup and inhaled the cool, night air. She wasn't in a particular hurry. The idiot man would survive a lone bat until she got there. It was a beautiful night—clear, with a canopy of bright stars sparkling overhead. She loved living on a lake. It made the air smell cleaner, fresher. Tree frogs trilled in the low, marshy area where a stream emptied into the lake.

When she parked by Ian's front door, he opened it and motioned her inside. He was in his pajama bottoms, too. Nothing more. *Lord have mercy.* How could a man look so good? She bit her bottom lip, trying to concentrate.

"Aren't you chilly without a shirt?" she asked.

"My chest of drawers is in the bedroom. The bat's diving all over in there. They go for your hair, don't they?"

He had wonderful hair—crisp and wavy—but Tessa doubted a bat would find it comfy.

He dragged her inside. "It's a fruit bat, right? You don't have any vampire bats around here?"

She rolled her eyes. What the hell did people who lived on the coasts read about the Midwest? "The werewolves ate all the vampire bats," she told him. "You're safe."

He scowled. He obviously didn't appreciate Midwest humor. "I called Bigfoot to help me, but he was busy. How do I get rid of it?"

She held up her tennis racket. "This way, we won't hurt it. We love bats around here. One bat eats tons of insects—like mosquitoes."

"I'll thank it later, once it's out of my house." He led her to his bedroom. She grimaced. Unoriginal—black comforter and sheets, dark furniture.

"It's from my apartment," he said. "You can help me make it look better, right?"

Tessa shook her head. "Not me, that's Lily's job." The bat swooped overhead, and Ian flinched. It finally clung to a rafter to rest.

Tessa stepped out of her sandals and looked at Ian. "Do you mind if I stand on your bed?"

"That's a new position, but whatever turns you on."

It was her turn to scowl. "Open the bedroom door, wide, shut every other door you can, and open both of your double doors. We'll see if I can wave this guy outside."

Ian hurried to do as she said. When he was finished, he called, "All ready."

She climbed on the bed, stood on tiptoe, and tapped the rafter the bat clung to. The bat took off, and she swung the racket behind him. After a few failed attempts, the bat flew out of the bedroom. She hurried after it, shutting the door behind her and swinging the racket, high in the air, until the bat flew down the hallway and into the great room. The ceiling soared there, and the bat flew in circles, high above her head.

She pulled out a chair to stand on. She swung some more, hoping the movement would agitate the bat. Her top kept riding up, and she had to yank it lower. Thank the heavens, she'd put on a bra. The bat flew toward the fireplace, and she stretched a little too much to make it change direction. Ian hurried to grab her waist when her chair started to tip. His hands gripped her firmly to hold her steady. Her top rose again, and his fingers touched bare skin. Frissons of pleasure rippled through her body.

A half hour later, the bat swooped out the front doors. Tessa sagged on her chair, her arms tired from so much waving.

Still supporting her, Ian circled to face her, a look of triumph on his face. "You did it!" As he lowered her to the floor, her breasts brushed his bare chest. Electricity shot through Tessa's body. She hadn't been so aware of a man in a long time. He felt her body tense and his responded. He pulled her slightly closer. His gaze fastened on her lips. Too much temptation. She was wading in murky waters. She motioned to the open doors. "Better shut those before the bat comes back in."

He jerked away from her and hurried to slam them closed. When he returned, his gaze looked as lust-filled as hers must. He tossed a teasing smirk her way. "And how did *you* get such great abs?"

The familiar blush crept to her cheeks. "I swim in good weather. I do crunches in winter, and I work in the yard. A girl can't just sit on her ass all day, writing."

"And you hide all that gloriousness under baggy shirts?"

She shrugged. "I'm not looking, remember?"

He shook his head. "Such a shame. You deserve someone wonderful. I know you got hurt once, but honestly, Tessa, some man would do cartwheels for winning the jackpot if he caught you."

"Not gonna happen. He'll have to look for another prize."

Ian looked genuinely upset. "You're depriving yourself and some, poor sap of something wonderful."

Tessa struggled to keep her gaze off his naked torso. She felt warm. Did women have hot flashes at her age? "No one said life was fair. I . . . and the sap will live." She started to the door. The sooner she got out of there, the better. "I have a big day tomorrow. So do you. Lily's coming. We both need sleep. See you on Monday."

Short, terse sentences. That's all she could manage. She hurried to her pickup and cussed herself on the drive home. She should have worn coveralls with a baggy shirt under them. Her mind said she wasn't interested in men, but her body didn't get the message. She was going to have to be careful around Ian.

Once back in her own bedroom, she looked in the mirror. Wild, copper hair spilled over her shoulders. Her eyes were too wide, too worried. Was this what had happened to Gary and Sadie? Had they been thrown together, living in the same apartment building, until their willpower proved too weak?

She pointed at her reflection. "I am not Sadie." She would never steal some other woman's man. As if she could. But that didn't matter. She was stronger than that, had more resolve.

Once her head hit the pillow, though, thoughts of Ian swam in her dreams.

Chapter 11

Friday morning came too early. Tessa groaned as she pushed herself out of bed. Damn Ian and his abs . . . no, his bats. She did her best to tame her hair, brushed on some mascara, and called it a day.

Grams took one look at her and grinned. "Did someone have a big night?"

Tessa explained about Ian's phone call. Grams laughed about rescuing him from a bat. Tessa left out everything else—how cute Ian looked with his dark hair all messy, what a gorgeous body he had, and how his touch made her think staying celibate was overrated.

Grams cocked her head while Tessa talked, though, and a knowing look crossed her face.

"Don't get any ideas," Tessa said. "He's taken."

"But at least he's getting your hormones working again. I thought they'd dried up."

Tessa huffed. "I still look, but I try not to touch."

"I miss that." Grams finished checking the money for change in her cash register.

"Miss what?" Tessa closed her cash drawer, too.

"Being touched. A hug, a nuzzle—touch is good."

Tessa turned and gave her a warm embrace.

"I love ya, kid, but it's not the same."

Tessa's eyes went wide with surprise. "You miss having a man?"

Grams' expression turned naughty. "I wouldn't get married this time around. We'd just live together."

Tessa gasped, and Grams laughed.

"After all, I don't have to worry about getting pregnant."

"Grandma!"

Thankfully, the first customers walked through the door, and things got so busy, they didn't get a chance to do anything but work. When they turned the sign over to CLOSED and locked the door, Tessa looked at the glass case and shook her head.

"I need to bake more German chocolate pies."

"Want some help?" Grams didn't sound sincere. Knowing Grams, she probably had plans to meet someone in town for supper.

It was nice of Grams to offer, but Tessa shook her head. "It won't take me that long. I have pie dough in the refrigerator, and the filling's a cinch to make."

"If you're sure."

Tessa shooed her away. It had been a long enough day for Grams, and she'd be here again tomorrow. "Get going."

Tessa finished straightening up the shop, then went to the kitchen and flopped on a stool. First, she'd take a break. Her stomach rumbled. She wanted more than a few cookies for supper. Saturday meant leftovers, and she had plenty of turkey dip left for a sandwich, but she'd eaten it for lunch enough times, it didn't appeal to her. She'd drive into town and grab something to-go from the diner.

It was a quick trip, but when she walked through the diner's doors, the first thing she saw was Ian, waving to her. Lily welcomed her with a smile, too.

"Come, sit with us!" Lily looked as wonderful, as always. Petite and bubbly, she had an infectious smile. She'd pulled her long, blonde hair into a high ponytail and wore jeans and a frilly top. Damn it all, she looked adorable.

Tessa felt like a copper frizz ball next to her. She walked to their table, but shook her head. "I called in for take-out. I'm grabbing my food and heading home. I ran out of German chocolate pies and have to bake more."

Lily wrinkled her nose. How cute could a girl get? Tessa tried not to hate her. "You have to work on a Friday night? That's horrible." She grinned. "I heard you rescued Ian from a big, bad bat last night."

Tessa smiled. "He'd have thought of something eventually. Either that, or they'd have made friends."

Ian shivered. He put a hand on Lily's shoulder. "We might stop at your bakery tomorrow so Lily can see it. My girl has a sweet tooth. You should probably hide things so she doesn't buy out the store."

Lily turned and pressed her forehead against his cheek. "He loves to tease me, but I do crave desserts. I have to be careful, though. I have to watch my figure."

"Everyone else does." Ian smiled up at Tessa. "Thanks for telling me about the diner. It's great. We thought we'd stick around town this weekend and get to meet some people." A smart move. People already liked him. They'd like him even more if he became part of the community. He settled his arm around Lily's shoulder, but leveled a look at Tessa "We'll see you tomorrow."

Oh, goodie. Tessa pushed away her snarky thoughts and went to collect her take-out. What did that look mean? A challenge? Speculation? On the drive home, she argued with herself. How much lovey-dovey could she stand? She shrugged. What difference did it make? She'd sworn off men. Lily could paw Ian in public if she wanted to, and vice-versa. It was nothing to her.

As she whizzed by Ian's place on her way home, she noticed the end of a flatbed truck parked almost out of view behind his house. Strange. Ian wouldn't hire workers for a project when Lily was here. She backed-up and turned into Ian's drive. When she got close enough to recognize the truck, she cussed softly to herself.

She pulled her cell phone out of her pocket and got out to investigate. When she saw Ned Cooper trying to pry open Ian's back door with a crowbar, she cleared her throat.

Ned whirled to see who was there. When he saw Tessa, he grimaced. He looked at the phone in her hand. "Are you gonna call Sheriff Brickle to turn me in?"

"What the hell are you doing, Ned?"

He dropped his crowbar and hung his head. "Sam promised he'd sell his place to me when he left town. He swore on his honor. Then he got a better offer from a stranger and signed the deal without one word to me. This should be my property, Tessie girl. Do you know how many favors I did for that man?"

Tessa's heart ached. She'd known Ned Cooper her whole life. He was a friend of her grandpa's. "Sam could be a real bastard. We all knew that, but you're mad at him, not Ian. You're not being fair."

"I just want what should be mine. I only wanted to drive him away."

"He's not going to leave, and he's going to be good for Mill Pond. What did you want to do with the property?"

Ned shrugged. "I've always wanted to wake up, look out my window, and see the water."

Tessa could understand that, but she shook her head. "You're too old to take on this much property. Why don't you buy a small cottage?"

Ned grinned. "You never did mince words, missy. But you're right. I'm just being mule-headed because Sam promised me a good deal." He looked at her cell phone again. "What now?"

"I'm not calling Brickle, but I am telling Ian. You cost him a lot of time and work. You can think up some kind of deal to make it up to him, but promise me you won't bother him again."

Ned sighed. "You got my word on it. And I just might start looking for a fishing cabin farther down on the point. Are you mad at me, Tessie?"

"I'm not happy with you, but you're the first person who taught me how to wet my line and bait a hook. I can't stay mad too long."

He patted her arm. "I'll be getting myself home then, and you don't have to worry about me anymore. Thanks, girlie."

Ned would be true to his word. Tessa climbed in her pickup and started for her place. She had a mind to call Sam Dramer and cuss him out, but it wouldn't change anything. She decided to put the whole thing behind her, grateful Ian wouldn't have to worry about any more vandalism.

She carried her food into the barn's kitchen and poured herself a glass of wine. She turned on the sound system and listened to music while she ate, then made another dozen pies. That was her limit tonight. If she ran out tomorrow, so be it. A nasty thought drifted through her mind. If she ran out of anything, she hoped it was one of Lily's favorites.

She went to bed soon after she stepped inside her house. When her alarm rang on Saturday, she woke, feeling rested. She spent more time than usual getting ready for the day. She dried her hair with a diffuser so that it bounced and curled. She applied more makeup than she normally did—eyebrow pencil, mascara, eyeliner, foundation, and blush. Her sprinkling of freckles still showed, but not as much. She even added a soft shade of lipstick.

She pulled on her best jeans and reached for a T-shirt, then decided on an aqua-blue, clingy, rayon shirt. She was heading to the barn when Luther and Kayla walked to meet her. "You know the routine," she told Luther. She handed him their spring check-off list. "Train Kayla for what she's going to do, and I'll see you later."

Luther gave a rare smile. "I've started working two nights a week at Lakeview Stables. It's a big place, but I got it all mowed."

She could hear the pride in his voice. "Ian got lucky, finding you."

"It's because you took the time to teach me. I'll teach Kayla. You'll see. We'll get everything done you need done." Luther took Kayla's hand and led her toward the garden beds. Tessa glanced at her watch and hurried to the barn.

Grams raised her eyebrows when she slid in the back door. "Hey, kid, you clean up good."

Tessa rolled her eyes, but the compliment lifted her spirits. Maybe she should try to look a little spiffier on workdays.

"I saw Luther," Grams said. "That boy looks like the cat that swallowed the canary."

"You're partial to him, you know."

"I like his girl, too. They're going to make us proud." Grams had always had a soft spot for Luther, but then Grams was the type who took in strays. Any cats or people that no one wanted and who showed up on her doorstep were lucky if they ever got to leave.

"I like Kayla," Tessa agreed. "She's a no-nonsense, practical girl."

"Luther doesn't like Ian's fiancée," Grams said, "doesn't like being around her."

"Why?"

"He says she's too happy. He doesn't trust her."

"What's wrong with being too happy?" Other than it made Tessa jealous as hell. She stiffened. No, that had to be a random thought. She wasn't jealous. Couldn't be. But Lily was the type of girl who made her feel inadequate every time they met.

Tessa struggled with the image of Ian and Lily, twisted in his sheets, sweaty and exhausted. *Oh, hell.* She pushed the image away. Damn the gorgeous, blonde bitch. *What was wrong with her?* She took a deep breath. "Well, we'd better turn the sign to OPEN. A line's forming." And a good thing, too. She needed to distract herself.

Grams and Tessa took their places behind the cash registers and dealt with one customer after another. Tessa looked up every time the door opened, but Ian and Lily never showed up. She felt silly for dressing up this morning. She felt silly for feeling disappointed when it wasn't Ian who walked through the door. Things were finally slow-ing down when Jed Mulgrew stood before her with the last sugar cream pie in his possession.

"This is the last one," he told her. "I'm taking it to the church carry-in tomorrow morning." Jed lived two towns over from Mill Pond. He was medium height with a stocky build and preferred to wear camouflage pants and plaid flannel shirts. A horrible combination.

"Your church is having a get-together, too?" Tessa asked. "Grams' church is putting on an ice cream social."

He shrugged. "We do it once a month. Your pie will be the best thing there. The women at our church aren't that great of cooks. Maybe Methodists are better, but Catholics go for volume. You never leave hungry."

Tessa blinked. In her mind, church carry-ins were always awesome with casseroles and desserts that made her drool. She frowned at Jed. "I've never been to a bad carry-in."

"You're lucky. Ours are nothing to brag about."

Tessa smiled. "You guys have bigger families. Maybe the women cook so much for their families, they're not in the mood to whip something up on Saturday night."

He repeated his shrug. "Could be, but I'm not looking forward to it. If I skip, though, Mom will kill me. Church is a big deal for her."

Tessa knew Jed's parents. Church was a big deal for his entire family. Growing up, she'd only sat in a pew with her family at Christmas and Easter. She handed Jed his pie. "Well, enjoy the company. You'll be with friends."

He tilted his head, squinted at her. "You look nice today. Would you like to go get a burger with me tonight, then finish at the mini-golf range?"

Normally, she'd say no. Normally, she'd run for the hills, but she needed something to distract her from Lily spending the weekend with Ian. She smiled. "Sure, why not?"

Grams looked at her like she was nuts.

Jed hurried to add, "We can't make it a late night. I have to get up for church tomorrow, and I can't have a hangover."

Tessa shrugged. Better and better. She didn't want to spend too much time with Jed. She was only dipping her toes in the water. "Okay."

He looked relieved. "I'll pick you up at seven. Will that work?"

"Fine with me." She didn't have high hopes for this date. But she'd get a free hamburger that she didn't have to cook. And she wouldn't be sitting at home.

"See you at seven," he repeated and left the shop.

Grams blinked at Tessa. "Really? Jed Mulgrew? He probably watches pond scum grow for entertainment."

"You told me I should start getting out again."

"You and Jed have about as much in common as Mickey Mouse and Angelina Jolie."

Tessa stared. "What do you know about Angelina Jolie?"

"She's edgy with a lot of tattoos. Mickey would be out of his league."

Tessa chuckled. "I thought I'd start with something safe."

Grams shook her head. "Safe doesn't even describe it. You could grow mold by the time you did anything exciting."

Tessa scowled, so Grams let it go.

After they closed up shop, Tessa had an hour before Jed came for her. She changed into a red, form-fitting top. Usually, red didn't compliment copperheads, as Grams called her, but this shade did. She added more foundation and blush, and even a new layer of lip gloss. More bother than she'd gone to for a while.

Jed looked her up and down when she came to the door. "You look pretty."

"Thanks." It had been a while since she'd fiddled with makeup. The response had been good.

He motioned her to his pickup truck. He didn't hold the door or help her with the high, step-up into his cab. He got behind the wheel and said, "Boy, I'm hungry. Can't wait for a burger."

They went to the bar on the edge of Mill Pond. Motorcycles lined its front parking spaces. Pickups filled the lot. Jed walked ahead of her to lead her inside. He nodded at Chase Carlton, the owner and bartender, and took a seat at the bar.

Chase trotted to take their orders. In his early thirties, Chase sported blond hair and stubble. He looked Tessa up and down. "Hey, farmer girl, you're lookin' good tonight."

She shook her head. "I didn't expect this place to be so busy."

"It's always busy on Saturdays, darlin'. You just wouldn't know because you don't come in here to make my night."

Jed laughed. "Like you need that. You never walk out of here alone, do you?"

Chase looked hurt. "Is it my fault ladies need someone to lift their spirits?"

The band started playing, and his words were drowned by noise. Tessa glanced at the family room on the far side of the building. The music didn't blast as loud there. She might be able to hear someone if they talked. Which Jed didn't. They ordered, they ate, and he paid. Then, he looked at her. "Ready for mini-golf?"

Not really, but she smiled. She'd grown up in the country club. She'd taken golf lessons, tennis lessons, and was on the swim team. Mini-golf was for amateurs. She could probably kick Jed's ass, but this wasn't a competition, right? It was supposed to be fun.

As they stood to leave, Chase gave her a wide grin and a wink. "Come anytime, and I'll throw in a free drink."

Well, there you go. Who could resist that?

Jed drove to the local range with a windmill on the first course, a stream on the second, and other hurdles to the last hole. Jed insisted that she start first. She whipped through the windmill barriers in short time.

Jed hit his ball, and it reflected off the far side. He hit again, and it reflected back toward the beginning. Five hits later, he'd made it past the spinning blades of the windmill. Five more hits, and he sank his first ball.

Tessa bit the inside of her cheek and groaned. She'd never played with anyone this bad. On the second course, she whizzed through the obstacles and finished early. Jed's ball went in the water. He got it out and knocked it out of the course. He started again, and ended up in the water . . . again. Tessa thought she'd grab her hair and scream, but forced herself to stay calm, to smile. Eight hits over, Jed finally sank his putt.

Were the heavens mocking her? Were they laughing at her attempt to get into the dating scene again? By the last tee, she had to force herself not to take Jed's club and beat him with it.

Jed grew grumpier the longer they played. By the time he finished, he was none too friendly. "When I come here with friends, I usually win."

"You're kidding. How often do you come?"

"A few times a summer."

"That explains it."

He looked at Tessa. "You know, you seemed like a nice girl, pretty easygoing."

"Did I?" She squinted at him. *Bring it on.* She'd taken martial arts. She could kick his rear end from one side of Mill Pond to the other.

"You didn't tell me you were a damned golf pro."

She tried to keep the edge out of her voice. "You didn't tell me you'd never played before."

"I have," Jed said.

"Not enough." Was he mad at her because she'd won?

"I came here two weeks ago. I got first place."

"Were all of your friends drunk?"

He glared. "You're sort of a know-it-all, aren't you?"

She glared back. "Not really, but golf might not have been the right pick for us."

He shrugged and led her to his truck. Didn't open her door . . . again. On the way back to her place, he said, "I like your pies enough, I thought you might be worth marrying. Word is, you're a good cook. But I don't think we'd get along."

"Are we breaking up?" She wouldn't laugh. It wouldn't be kind.

"I'm sorry, Tessa. You're nice enough, but I can tell you're not from around here. You came from a big city. It shows."

She gave a grim nod, waited for him to drop her at her house, and then heaved a sigh of relief when he left. Then, she couldn't help it. She doubled over with laughter. There was a reason she preferred being single.

Chapter 12

The first Sunday in May started too early. Normally, Tessa slept in on Sundays. Grams gave her grief about that. Grams was a regular at the little church in town. Tessa read the newspaper, drank an entire pot of coffee by herself, and enjoyed not doing anything. Today, though, she had to be at Grams' church by eleven-thirty.

"Doll up a little," Grams told her. "This is about having fun."

Tessa stood in front of her closet and sighed. The best she could do was a flirty, summer skirt and a cute, white blouse with tiny buttons that ran its entire length. She pulled her hair back with a white ribbon, slipped gold earrings in her ears, and stepped into a pair of sandals with a small heel. She looked in the mirror and grimaced. It was as good as she got.

She gathered her four pie carriers—three for the dessert table and one for Garth Roarke. She knew he'd be at the social. A bachelor, Garth came to every food event in Mill Pond. She loaded the pies on the front seat of her pickup, and off she went.

Grams waved to her the minute Tessa stepped onto the front lawn of the church. "Over here!"

Tessa took the three pies to Hilda Svenson, who gave her an approving nod. A white-haired friend of Grams, Hilda had a sweet smile, a soft voice, and a will of iron. She was always in charge of the social, and she expected Tessa to show up with pies. Tessa wasn't brave enough to disappoint her.

That duty done, Tessa crossed the yard to Grams. Miguel Rodriquez stood, chatting with her. Tessa knew from experience that Grams and Miguel could spend entire afternoons debating which strawberry plants produced the most fruit and which dahlias bloomed best. They both had a passion for landscaping. So did she, but she didn't want to talk about plants and gardens all day.

"Hi, kid!" Grams eyes glowed with excitement. "Miguel was telling me about a new species of climbing roses that won Most Hardy in his horticulture magazines this spring."

"Really?" Tessa braced herself for an afternoon of high-octane entertainment—Not. She zeroed in to listen when someone grabbed her elbow and gave it a squeeze. Turning, she saw Keavin Neeley, one of her old, childhood buddies when she came to Mill Pond to stay with Grams and Gramps every summer.

He smiled from ear to ear when she turned to him. "Look who grew up."

Her heart melted at the sight of him. How long had it been? Since they both graduated from high school and went their separate ways. Damn, he looked as warm and friendly as always. The same height she was and slightly overweight, he reminded her of a cuddly teddy bear, but there was a thick streak of orneriness in there somewhere. "You still look like trouble."

He laughed and pulled her to him for a hug. She was laughing, too, when she looked over his shoulder and saw Ian and Lily walking toward a half-empty table. Ian's face looked like a storm ready to happen. His gaze shot darts at her. *What the hell?*

"Looks like I'm making your boyfriend jealous," Keavin teased.

"Not my boyfriend. Engaged. I'd guess he's had an argument with Lily."

Tessa waved as Darinda and David moved down a seat to make room for Ian and his fiancé. The minute they were seated, people wandered over to greet them. With one last scowl her way, Ian turned, and his ready smile lit his face.

Keavin watched, amused. "No, that look was meant for you. You've pissed him off royally, but if I remember right, you were good at that."

"Not fair! I'm a true and loyal friend."

Keavin chuckled and pushed her away. His crooked grin turned into a goofy smile. "I always knew you were going to turn into a real beauty when you grew up."

Tessa rolled her eyes. "You haven't gotten any smarter with age."

"Didn't need to. I was plenty smart to begin with." He put an arm around her shoulders and tugged her toward the grills, filled with hot dogs. "I'm claiming her, Grams!" he called. "You see her all the time."

Grams waved them off and returned her attention to Miguel.

Lily's voice drifted to them as Ian introduced her to Evan Meyers and his wife. "You raise goats? I flew here from Mexico. They eat goats there."

Evan's brows rose, and he looked surprised. "We raise them for milk and cheese."

"Evan's farm is listed on a foodie tour for the area," Darinda said, and the conversation flowed to area attractions.

Tessa tuned out Lily and leaned into Keavin in comfortable companionship. "What have you been up to since you left Mill Pond for college?"

"A little bit of everything. I took journalism, like I planned, and then I traveled a lot. Now, I write for businesses and magazines."

"That was always your dream."

Keavin looked at her, smiling. A strand of copper hair escaped her ribbon, and he smoothed it back behind her ear. "I'm thinking of coming back to the Midwest to work for a newspaper in one of the cities."

"Because you missed the cows and corn?"

He laughed. "No, because Dad's been diagnosed with cancer. Mom's not handling it too well, and I'm getting married in a few weeks. Chelsea doesn't want to raise our kids in a big city."

Lily's voice carried to them again. "Your lake's beautiful, but it can't compare with the Caribbean. The water's so perfect."

Tessa glanced over her shoulder to see Grams and Miguel, talking with Lily. The whole town was making an effort to make her feel welcome. Tessa reached to hug Keavin. "I'm sorry about your dad, but I'm happy you've found someone. You'll make a great husband and dad."

"Yeah, keep telling me that. I might believe it. I don't know how I tricked Chelsea into falling for me." He looked at her. "And you? How are you and Gary?"

"We didn't last. I'm not in any hurry to find someone new."

He frowned, studying her. "You know what? I'm not worried. Some guy's going to swoop down and carry you away someday. And you're going to like it."

"If you say so." As they stood in line to get hotdogs and potato salad, she heard Lily again.

"I just spent an entire week in Greece. Mediterranean cuisine is heaven."

Keavin raised an eyebrow. "That girl should put on a slide show. Then we'd all know what a jet-setter she is."

"She's not too bad. I think she's just nervous." They got their food and went to find a table. They found an empty one and sat down.

Everyone came to say hello. People hadn't seen Keavin in a long time. They all had stories to tell about how rambunctious he was as a kid.

Between hotdogs and desserts, people traded tables, trying to make the rounds. When Keavin and Tessa searched for a place to sit, David waved them over.

Darinda stood to give Keavin a hug. "Long time, no see."

Before Keavin could respond, Gianni and Luigi charged to the table, licking cones filled with strawberry ice cream. "Taste it, Tessa! It's homemade," Gianni said. He pushed it toward her, smooshing ice cream on the tip of her nose. "It has real strawberries. We got to crank the handle."

Tessa took a lick and reached for his cone. "Delicious."

Giggling, Gianni pulled it back, guarding it for himself.

"Are these yours?" Keavin wiped the ice cream off Tessa's nose with his napkin.

Tessa laughed. "Silly question. Just look at them!" Both boys had their mother's tight, black curls.

"David and I have to claim them. They look like us." Darinda motioned toward Ian and Lily to introduce them. "Ian bought Sam Draper's place, and he's making it into a resort."

Keavin held out a hand for a quick shake. "That's a perfect spot for something like that." And the talk turned to what Ian was doing on his property.

Tessa listened to the ebb and flow of the conversation, only half concentrating. It was a beautiful day. Big, puffy clouds dotted a blue sky. A slight breeze made things comfortable. Laughter filtered to them, and Tessa took a deep breath of contentment.

"Right, Tess?" Keavin turned to her. She blinked, and he laughed. "Just like always, wool gathering." He put a hand under her chin and rubbed his knuckles over the top of her head. "A noogie for not paying attention."

She gave an absent smile, remembering their childhood antics. She'd gotten many a noogie in her time.

"You're too old for that," Darinda protested.

"I'll never be too old to pester Tess." Keavin wrapped his arm around her shoulders again.

Ian's expression turned murderous. What was his problem?

Darinda grimaced. "You two!"

Ian's eyes narrowed, and Lily turned to look at him, a thoughtful expression on her face. Just then, Tessa spotted Garth and Leona walking to a table.

Tessa pulled on Keavin's shirt. "Come on. I see Garth. I brought him a pie."

"What kind of a pie?" Keavin's tone was plaintive.

"Oh, stop! I'll bake you one. Your favorite—pumpkin."

He let her pull him to his feet to go see Garth. By the time they returned, Ian grinned up at her, relaxed. Lord, he was moody today.

Darinda looked smug. What the hell had happened while she was gone? Tessa looked from one person to the other as she and Keavin took their seats.

Darinda locked gazes with her as she told Keavin, "Ian was asking about your line of work."

Tessa frowned, confused. Subtleties were ebbing and flowing around her, and she didn't have a clue what they meant.

Keavin leaned forward, always ready to talk shop. "Are you interested in journalism?"

Ian smiled. "No, sorry, I'd just never heard anyone mention you before. In this town, everyone seems to know everyone else. It surprised me that your name hadn't come up."

"This is the first time I've been back in a while," Keavin told him. "Thought I'd catch up on old times and pick the brain of a fellow writer." He bumped Tessa's shoulder. "The girl's made a name for herself, and I could use a few pointers."

Ian's glare returned. "She's famous?"

"She's no Nora Roberts, but she's doing okay for herself." Keavin laughed. "I wouldn't mind selling like she does."

"Are you thinking of writing a book?" Tessa asked him.

"It's crossed my mind."

Tessa lit up. There were few things in life she enjoyed as much as talking to a fellow writer.

"Oh, no." Darinda groaned. "She's going into writing mode. We might as well disappear." She stood and started gathering their plates and napkins. David rose, too, to help her.

"Is it that bad?" Ian asked.

"You might as well be invisible. Trust me. These two will have their heads together for another hour."

Lily tugged on Ian's arm. "You promised to show me around the town."

"Is there anything here that would interest you? We can't compete with Greece or the Caribbean."

She gave a cute moue. "I went a little overboard, didn't I?"

"A little?"

She tugged at him again. "You promised."

"I did, didn't I?" He looked up and down the town square. "We can window shop, but a lot of the shops are closed on Sundays."

"Why?" Lily stared.

"It's a Midwest thing." Ian crooked his elbow for her, and they set off to look at the shops. When they returned an hour later, Tessa was saying goodbye to Keavin and gathering her pie carriers to load in her truck. Almost everyone else had gone.

Lily grabbed Ian's hand and followed Tessa to her pickup. "Why don't you go help those poor men carry the last folding tables into the church?" she told Ian.

He hurried to help them.

Lily turned to Tessa. "People seem really nice here," she said.

Tessa dropped the plastic carriers on her front seat. "Every town has a squirrely person or two, but Mill Pond is a friendly community, as a whole."

"People seem pretty open-minded, too." Lily's blue eyes sparkled.

Tessa nodded. What was she maneuvering toward? "We're pretty middle-of-the-road. Not too conservative, not too liberal."

Lily's lips curved into a smile. "Good, because I've been a little worried about my Ian. I travel a lot, and I don't want him to get lonely."

"He's made lots of friends here," Tessa assured her.

"I'm sure he has, but that's not the same, is it?"

"The same as what?"

"Ian's really fond of you, I can tell. If you two would ever like to spend more time together"—Lily hesitated—"to enjoy each other's company, it wouldn't bother me."

Tessa stared. Was she suggesting what she thought she was suggesting? She felt a blush burn to her hairline. "I couldn't do that."

"He's one of the good ones. If you change your mind, I'm fine with it."

Tessa glanced across the yard at Ian. "I don't think he'd be okay with it either."

"I'll talk to him," Lily said.

"No, don't. I really . . . couldn't."

Lily smiled. "If you say so, but I thought I'd offer."

"Well, um, thanks." Tessa didn't know what else to say. Ian finished with the chairs and started toward them. He caught her expression and hesitated. Before he could return to them, she jumped inside her pickup and sped away.

Chapter 13

On Monday, Tessa woke to the sound of rain, dancing on her roof. She stretched under her blankets. She couldn't work outside, so she burrowed deeper into her pillow, letting herself enjoy an extra few minutes before getting out of bed.

It was May, the first day she'd open the farm stand, but she doubted there'd be much business. Who'd come to buy fresh lettuce or spinach in this weather? She padded down the oak steps to the kitchen and poured herself a cup of coffee. Carrying it to the kitchen window, she watched the steady drizzle water her flowerbeds. Luther and Kayla's cabin would be empty right now while they were in school. Had Luther told Kayla she didn't need to show up for work on rainy days? Tessa would have to mention it. She spent six days a week in the barn during the busy season and could cover the stand on days when there wouldn't be many customers. Either that, or Kayla could work inside with her when the stand was slow. That might be a better idea.

By the end of the month, Luther and Kayla would graduate. Thank goodness. Tessa would need help by then. Strawberries would be ripe enough to pick. There'd be pies and jams to make. Raspberries, blackberries, and blueberries . . . she sighed. Spring and summer meant long days.

She poured a second cup of coffee and carried it to her bedroom to drink. She pulled on her old, faded jeans and her yellow T-shirt, spotted with food stains—her cooking clothes. She never bothered with an apron when she wore these.

She rinsed out her coffee cup, then flipped open her umbrella, and started to the barn. She'd spend the day mixing cookie dough to freeze. It would be ready when she needed it. She might as well make a few batches of pie dough, too.

She slowed her steps as rain drops bounced off her umbrella. Aah, the smell of spring showers. The air she breathed invigorated. In the summer, she and Darinda used to run wild in the warm rain, but it was too early in the year for that. Still too cold.

Once she reached the barn's back door, her gym shoes squished as she walked. She popped them off and put them on a newspaper by the door, then went barefoot as she gathered the ingredients she needed. When she passed the stainless steel refrigerator, she caught a glimpse of her hair. Holy, Medusa! It was sticking out everywhere. She sliced off a piece of cooking twine and wrestled the curls back in a ponytail.

An hour later, she had three mixers going when someone pounded on the door. She'd hung a sign at the farm stand, IF YOU NEED SOME-THING, KNOCK AROUND BACK. Everyone in the area knew her routine. She hurried to meet a customer. Ian stood there, soaking wet.

She stared at him. "Didn't you bring an umbrella?"

"If I had, don't you think I'd use it?" He pushed past her into the warm room. She had pie shells baking in the ovens for future use, and he rubbed his arms, clearly enjoying the heat. "I went to your house first and figured you weren't home, but I saw your pickup in the garage, so thought you were probably out here. I knocked on the shop door for forever, but you didn't answer, so I finally came back here."

"You didn't see my sign?" But then, it was hung at the stand, not the bakery. She motioned to the mixers. "I couldn't hear you over the noise."

"I noticed." His tone was a bit snippy. His dark hair was plastered to his head, and his white T-shirt was glued to his body. He glanced at her wet shoes, sitting on a newspaper by the door, and stepped out of his shoes, too, leaving them on the paper beside hers. "We need to talk."

He didn't come any farther into the room. A puddle formed where he was standing. She took pity on him, looked under the island's counter, and handed him a roll of paper towels. "Dry yourself off." She went to the bathroom and tossed him a hand towel to stand on.

He dabbed and rubbed until he didn't drip anymore. His shirt still clung to him, though. He gave her a questioning look. *Oh, hell, why not?* The wet shirt was just as sexy as his bare abs. When she shrugged, he pulled it over his head and tossed it on top of his shoes.

Oh, crap, you'd think she'd get used to seeing him, half-naked, that maybe she'd grow immune to it. *Seen one set of great abs, you've seen them all.* Except his were wonderful.

The heavens were mocking her. That had to be it. They were testing her resolve. Well, she'd show them. Bare chested men didn't interest her.

Ian walked closer to the oven. His jeans clung to his legs, too. When he looked at her, she scowled. She had her limits. If his underwear was as wet as his pants, she didn't want to see what it clung to. His lips curved in a smile, as though he'd read her thoughts. But the poor man was soaked.

She held up a finger and went to the bathroom again. This time, she returned with a beach towel. After all, the lake was only a short distance away. In the summer, she zipped outside after a few hours of baking and jumped in the water to cool off.

He wrapped it around his waist, knotted it, then unzipped his jeans. They dropped on top of his T-shirt. The towel sagged lower on his torso, and Tessa handed him a long apron. Grinning, he slid the ties over his head.

She grimaced at his wet clothes. They'd never dry in a soggy pile. She pulled chairs behind the ovens and draped them there.

She shook her head at Ian. What a sight! A flowered apron and a bright-colored beach towel. She'd take a picture, but if she posted it online, women would probably send Ian all sorts of indecent proposals.

She flipped off her mixers, one by one, and the kitchen suddenly grew too quiet. She raised her eyebrows at him. "You braved the rain. Is everything okay?"

"It's too wet to get any outside work done today," he told her. "We need to talk. I saw the look on your face before you left the ice cream social. Lily told me what she said to you."

Tessa chewed on her bottom lip. "I asked her not to."

"Lily's not the type to keep secrets, spills whatever she knows, but that's the dumbest idea she's come up with yet." He shook his head. His hair was drying in soft waves. "I don't know what the hell she was thinking."

Neither did Tessa. If she had Ian, she wouldn't share. But Tessa didn't want to think about that. She waved the whole idea away. "Maybe it was a test, to see if either of us would take her up on it."

He scowled. "Lily likes her freedom. She travels from place to place, and she spent time with a lot of different men before she met me. When we started getting serious, we argued about that, and I was ready to walk."

"So she changed?"

"I can do the dating scene or the monogamous. But I'm not into monogamous with free passes on the side. Lily thought you might tempt me enough to rethink that."

Tessa frowned. "She still wants other guys on the side? That's still her preference?"

"Yeah, makes me sound special, doesn't it?"

"And you're okay with that?"

"Hell, no. She knows if she sees someone else, I'm done. She swears I'm worth hanging onto, but that doesn't mean she's above trying to maneuver things to get her own way."

Tessa's thoughts whirled in a jumble. At least Gary didn't want to have both her *and* Sadie. Why didn't it bother Ian that he wasn't enough, on his own, to satisfy Lily?

He shrugged. "I'm not thrilled with it, okay? But so far, Lily's kept her end of the bargain, and the longer we're together, the more I think she's going to settle down. I gave her the option of calling things off, and she started crying." He winced. "I'm the one who wanted to get serious, and she's trying. I have to give her that."

"But you're going to marry her? That's long term."

"I know." He rubbed his forehead, as though trying to massage away a headache. "So does Lily."

Tessa wasn't so sure. "I trusted Gary, and it was a mistake. But maybe you're right. Lily's flying in to see you every weekend. She wants to make things work with you."

He sighed. "That's what makes it so hard."

"Makes what so hard?" Tessa wasn't following him.

"It doesn't matter." Ian's expression turned serious. "I'm sorry she put you through that. It had to make you feel . . . weird."

"Weird." She tasted the word. "That's a good way to describe it."

"Well, I'm sorry it happened." He looked around the kitchen, sniffed the air. "What are you making?" It was obvious he wanted to move to a different topic.

She explained about making cookie and pie dough ahead for days when she was too busy during the summer.

"Need some help?" He grinned. "I used to love helping my mom in the kitchen."

"I'm going to be here all day. You don't have anything you need to do?"

"There's always something to do. You run a business. You know how it goes, but I feel like playing hooky."

A helping hand would make the work go faster. She handed him the right-sized, ice cream scoop. "Why not?"

She stirred walnuts and chocolate chips into the first batch of cookie dough, then showed him how to scoop it onto the parchment-covered baking sheets. Once they finished that batch of cookies, she put them in the oven. When the cookies cooled, she'd freeze them. Then she filled a plastic baggie with sugar and cinnamon. When she dropped a ball of the snickerdoodle dough into the bag, she looked up and caught Ian scraping his finger around the inside of the first, empty bowl.

He shrugged. "What can I say? I'm a professional bowl licker."

"I can see that." No wonder he helped his mother. But then, when she was little, she stole whole chunks of dough before Grandma could bake her cookies.

After Ian had gotten every bit of dough he could, he helped her with the snickerdoodles. She didn't bake those. She froze the individual balls of dough instead. Later, she'd put them in a big freezer bag, when they wouldn't stick together. For the chocolate crinkle cookies, she scooped all of the dough into a large bag and sealed it before putting it in the freezer. The dough was too messy to handle unless it was ice-cold.

Ian dutifully licked every bowl and spoon. Then they washed all the utensils and started again. By the time they finished, Tessa had frozen peanut butter, date pinwheel, and oatmeal raisin cookies. Ian had forced himself to sample one of each—for quality control—and approved them all. Tessa now had frozen pie shells and frozen pie dough, too. It had been a long day, but she was happy with what she'd gotten done. More, she'd discovered once she plugged into work mode, Ian didn't tempt her. Either that, or she didn't fall for guys in granny aprons and beach towels.

Ian glanced at the clock on the stove. "Boy, baking takes a lot more time than I thought. It's almost five." He patted his apron-clad stomach. "I'm starving."

Tessa bit her bottom lip. "Sorry, we should have stopped for lunch. When I start baking, I forget sometimes."

He laughed. "I ate so much dough, I didn't miss lunch, but my body's getting hungry for real food."

They did a final clean of the kitchen, and Ian slipped behind the empty ovens. He pulled on his dry T-shirt, mostly dry jeans, and then stepped into his shoes. Doggone it. The man looked almost as good dressed as he did mostly naked. The rain still pattered outside, so on the walk to the house, Tessa handed him her umbrella. They both huddled under it, jostling against each other. He felt good, too—all muscle and maleness.

"Lily's not flying in this coming weekend," he told her. "My brother's going to spend a few days with me so that I can show him around."

"You own a lodge. Isn't there enough space for both of them?"

"Brody and Lily don't get along."

Maybe Ian's brother wasn't a fan of bed-hopping. Good for him.

They dashed in the kitchen door of her house, and she frowned at him. "How are the guest rooms at your place? Almost finished?"

He followed her to the refrigerator and smiled when she took out a thick slice of ham. "Every room's painted. I bought king-sized beds for each room on the third floor; two, double beds for each room on the second. The chests of drawers are set up with flat-screen TVs over them. I wanted Lily to help me pick out comforters and decorations, but she doesn't like shopping for stuff like that." He looked at Tessa hopefully.

She shrugged. "We can probably find them online and have them delivered."

"Perfect." He helped her quarter potatoes and drop them in a pan of cold water. "What else?"

"I'll make the cole slaw if you cook the ham." She hauled a grill pan out of a bottom cupboard and placed it on two burners.

They worked in comfortable silence and then carried their plates to the three-season room to eat. A cool breeze blew through the open windows. Ian stretched his long legs and sighed. "This is nice."

When they finished eating, he rinsed and stacked their plates in the sink, while Tessa placed her laptop on the kitchen table. Ian drew up a chair, and they flipped through online pages to find the right comforters, towels, and throw pillows for his guest rooms.

"This is what I have, so far." He pulled out his cell phone and showed her a picture he'd taken of a room. The headboard and drawers looked like antique, white pieces. "I thought that would go with anything. I want each room to be unique."

They chose different colors and patterns for each room, then even hit art sites to look for paintings and posters. By the time Ian dashed out the door to his Mustang, he'd ordered all of the basics to finish the rooms.

Tessa stood on the front porch and watched him drive away. She gazed after him until his tail lights disappeared. She had to admit that she'd enjoyed his company a little too much today. Grams might be right, that she'd been alone a little too long. Maybe it was time to start circulating again, to start making herself available.

Chapter 14

The rest of the week flew by. Tessa planted snap peas, green beans, squash of every kind, eggplants, and more. By the time Grams came on Thursday, almost every garden bed was full.

"My mom never planted seeds until after Mother's Day," Grams said. "And she always went by the *Farmer's Almanac.*"

Tessa nodded. She'd heard this lecture over and over again. "I felt lucky this spring. Thought I'd take a chance."

Grams shook a finger. "You get antsy and plant too soon every year." Then she smiled. "But it's worked so far, so why not?"

Tessa waited for Grams to sprinkle flour on the granite counter to roll out pie dough before asking, "So, did you order the rose bushes Miguel was telling you about?"

"I didn't need to." Grams gave a small smile. "Miguel gave me two of them."

"He never gave you roses before."

"There's always a first time." Grams studied the recipe for banana cream pie. She'd made it a million times and knew it by heart.

Tessa narrowed her eyes. "What's the deal?"

"Miguel's taking me to the city for supper tonight."

"To the city?"

Grams nodded. "Two Q-tips on the town. Should be fun."

"Q-tips?"

"Oldsters with white hair."

Tessa stopped what she was doing to study her grandmother. Gramps had been gone a long time. Tessa had moved into the farmhouse when Grams moved into town. That was six years ago, and Gramps had died a couple years before that. She reached across the counter to pat her grandma's hand. "Have fun tonight."

"Thanks, hon. I was hoping you'd understand."

Tessa flipped on her stereo system, and she and Grams listened to big-band tunes while they baked. When they finished, and Grams was ready to leave, Tessa said, "Don't stay out too late. I can't handle the shop alone tomorrow morning."

"I'll tell Miguel to set his alarm." When Tessa's jaw dropped, Grams laughed.

Tessa locked up and walked to her house to find Ian sitting on the front porch, rocking in one of the wicker chairs.

"Brody's coming tomorrow afternoon," he told her as he followed her inside. "I can't wait for him to see the lodge."

"Did the comforters come?" The site had promised two-day shipping.

Ian nodded. "The rooms look great. I'll be open for business soon." He showed her a few more pictures on his phone. The wooden floors were dotted with rag rugs. Lace curtains hung at each window. Old-fashioned blinds with fringed hems shaded them. The rooms looked homey and welcoming.

Ian fidgeted through supper. He reminded her of Darinda's boys, too antsy to eat. She fidgeted, too. She needed to tell him about Ned and the vandalism, but she couldn't think of the right words. He wolfed down his bowl of chili, slopped up more with cornbread, and was ready to take off the minute they finished eating.

"I need to tell you something before you go." She'd tried to work up her courage over and over again, but hadn't managed. She didn't want to wait until his brother was here, so she squared her shoulders and the words spilled out. When she finished, she said, "Ned's a decent guy. He won't bother you again."

Ian narrowed his eyes and studied her. "You like him."

"He was one of my grandpa's close friends."

Ian shrugged. "Then we're good."

"Just like that?" She didn't expect Ned to get off so easy.

"You've done more than enough favors for me. I can do this for you."

She blinked, feeling a rush of emotions she didn't want to explore. "Thank you."

He grinned. "That's what neighbors are for. You keep telling me that."

She grinned, too. He was right.

He gave her a quick kiss on the cheek and took off.

The peace and quiet felt good. Tessa put her feet up and flipped on the TV. She'd watch a few shows to relax.

She woke in the morning, feeling stiff and sore. She'd fallen asleep on the couch and she had to rush to shower and dress for work. No time for makeup. The damp ends of her hair dried fuzzy, even though she'd pulled her hair up to shower. She wasn't going to win any beauty prizes today. She dashed inside the bakery just before the first customer arrived.

Grams laughed at her. "And you were worried about me."

"Sorry, I fell asleep on the couch." She glanced outside the door when a couple entered the shop. "Luther must have given up on me, but Kayla's already busy at the farm stand. And Luther's on the tractor, mowing. Guess they don't need me anymore."

Grams laid a hand on her shoulder. "That boy will always need you. Be good to him."

"No worries there."

The only worry for the rest of the day was trying to keep the line of people moving who came in and out of the shop. When the last customer left at five, she went to turn the sign in the door to CLOSED, but waited when Ian's Mustang pulled into the lot. She opened the door wider as he climbed out of his car and led his brother toward her. With a smile for both her and Grams, he said, "This is my older brother, Brody. He's staying at the lodge this weekend."

"Oh, lordy." Grams wiped her hands on the white apron that circled her waist.

Brody glowered down at her. Ian's brother was as tall as he was, but instead of an athletic build, he stood solid and strong. Like a bear. All bulging muscles. And instead of an easy smile, his expression looked forbidding—a warning to beware.

Grams was rarely at a loss for words, so Tessa stepped forward and held out a hand. "Welcome to Mill Pond."

Brody's smoky-gray eyes narrowed on her. "You must be Tessa. Ian said you were pretty. You are."

Tessa blinked. It sounded more like an affirmation of Ian's opinion than a compliment. "Thank you. How long are you staying?"

Brody glanced at his brother. "Only five days. I couldn't get away from work any longer than that."

Tessa tried to remember if Ian had mentioned what Brody did.

Brody supplied the answer. "I own a construction company. Spring and summer are our busy seasons."

Tessa nodded and looked to Ian. "Have you shown him the lodge?"

"He likes everything I've done." Ian's grin spread from ear-to-ear. "He came with me to look it over before I put in an offer and he approves of all the changes."

"That's because you helped him," Brody said. "I saw the chandeliers Lily picked out. Frilly for a lodge. You've made everything work."

Tessa tried to deflect the compliment. "That's because Ian and I like a lot of the same things. It made it easy."

Brody's frown made Tessa worry she'd said the wrong thing. She glanced to Ian for help, but he shook his head. "Brody and Lily don't get along. They usually avoid each other. I think you two are going to hit it off, though."

"Aaah!" She motioned to the empty cases. "I'd send you home with a cake or pie, but we sold out."

"Are all the cookies gone, too?" Ian sounded disappointed.

Tessa tilted her head toward the kitchen. "I have the frozen cookies we baked."

"Ian baked with you?" Brody crossed his arms over his chest.

Ian shrugged. "It was a rainy day. I didn't have anything else to do. Tessa let me lick the bowls."

"You run a business. There's always something to do."

"Nothing as important as licking bowls."

A smile softened Brody's expression. "Mom used to let us do that."

Ian raised his eyebrows at his brother. "If you're nice to Tessa, she might let *you* bake with her."

Brody's gray gaze turned on her. He studied her long enough that Tessa squirmed. Then he smiled. "I'd like that."

Oh, lordy. But Tessa dug deep to make him feel welcome. "I take it you like cookie dough, too?"

His whole face lit up. "Mom used to leave extra dough in the bowls for me. I was her favorite son."

"Were not!" Ian laughed. "But I'll take you up on the frozen cookies, Tessa."

She led them to the back of the barn and the kitchen. Grams quietly followed. What was up with her? Gramps always said that Grams would chat up the devil if he popped into her kitchen.

Ian halted at the granite-topped island and stared at the coffee cake, waiting there.

Tessa dug a bag of frozen, chocolate chip cookies out of the freezer and scooted both the bag and the coffee cake toward him.

"I couldn't." But he didn't sound very sincere.

"I baked it for you and Brody. I thought you might like it tomorrow morning."

Ian reached for it. "You sent a coffee cake home with me when I first moved here. Is this the same kind?"

She stared. "I don't remember what I gave you. I took it out of the freezer. This is a sour cream with streusel."

"I love streusel."

She smiled. "I know."

Brody tossed Ian a dark look. When Ian looked at him and said, "What?" Brody only shook his head.

Ian sighed. "Well, I think Brody's had all the fun he can stand. I'm going to drag him home."

She and Grams walked them to the shop door and watched them leave. The minute they were gone, Grams turned to Tessa. "I want one."

"He might be a little young for you."

"Then you have to marry him so I can look at him." Grams started cleaning the glass case.

Tessa grabbed the broom to sweep. "He's scary," she said. "Too intense for me."

Grams put away her dishrag and sighed. "When men like that soften up for a woman, it's like watching a flower bloom."

Tessa stared at her. "What did you do with my real grandma? She doesn't wax rhapsodic."

Laughing, Grams hung her apron on a peg and started for the door. "Talking about blooms, I have two, new roses, and Miguel is bringing supper to my place tonight, something he cooked."

"You're seeing him two nights in a row?"

"For enchiladas, I'd give him a foot massage," Grams said. "Maybe more. See ya, kid." And she was gone.

Tessa shook her head. Who knew Grams was such a wild child?

She took her time finishing up before she locked the barn and started to her house. Tomorrow was Sunday. Her day of rest. And then she remembered. Darinda and David were doing the carry-in to welcome Ian to Mill Pond. She'd already made the dessert, so all she had to do was show up and enjoy herself. But Brody would be there. And she'd feel like she had to be on her best manners.

She shrugged. *To hell with it.* She was tired. She walked home and crashed on the couch for the rest of the night.

Chapter 15

When Tessa walked into Darinda's house carrying tiramisu, Darinda whipped it out of her hands and placed it on the counter in the kitchen.

"I love you, girl!" Darinda wrapped her in a tight embrace. When the boys saw the bag of cookies in her hands, they came to hug her legs. That's when Ian and Brody walked through the door.

Brody raised his dark eyebrows at her. "You have a strange effect on people."

"Not me, my cooking."

Darinda released her and hurried to welcome Ian and his brother. She hugged Ian, then slowly looked Brody up and down. "Man, you're one daunting dude."

"I'll take that as a compliment."

Darinda frowned at the bare finger on his left hand. "No wedding ring? No woman's snagged you yet?"

"Divorced," Brody growled.

"Bitter and ugly?" Darinda was like that. She could ask impertinent questions in a breezy fashion and get away with it.

"Worse." Brody rolled his shoulders, as though unhappy even thinking about it.

"Well, you're among friends here. We love your brother." Darinda led them to the French doors that opened onto the back deck, where David manned the grill, and friends surrounded him. The deck's steps led down to a cement patio that circled a kidney-shaped pool. "We don't live on the lake, so we had to make do. Hope you brought your swimsuits."

"They're in the car. We got your message." Ian looked at Tessa. "Did you bring yours?"

She had, but she'd feel self-conscious wearing it in front of the two McGregor brothers. "I usually just hang out and yak with Darinda."

"But you brought it?" Ian persisted.

She sighed. "It's in my bag."

"Good, then we can dunk you." A sparkle lit his brown eyes. "That's a small bag. It must be a small suit."

"Will you stop it?" Darinda gave him a playful push. "Tess is stubborn enough, if you bug her, she digs in. Leave her alone."

Two arms circled Tessa from behind and Keavin's chuckle filled her ears. "Hey, Tessie!"

She didn't have to turn around to see who held her. She smiled. "You're still here?"

"I'll be around. I'm house shopping and staying with Mom and Dad for a while."

David called from the deck, "The chicken's ready, folks! Time to eat."

No one needed to be told twice. People grabbed plates and headed to the deck. Picnic tables had been lined up across the cement patio. Garth Roarke and Leona hurried in at the last minute, bearing three bottles of white wine.

Everyone loaded their plates, sipped drinks, and settled in for a good time. Ian and Brody sat across from Tessa and Keavin.

Brody scowled at him. "I'm Ian's brother. I heard you're getting married soon."

Keavin blinked, but nodded amiably. "In a few weeks. And you? How do you like Mill Pond? Are you thinking of moving to the area, too?"

"Not in the immediate future, my construction company's in upstate New York. But I like it here. Ian's found a good spot for a resort."

"Is your family in New York?" Keavin looked up and down the tables. "Most of the folks here have lived in Mill Pond all their lives."

Brody swallowed a bite of potato salad. "Our parents and two sisters all live near Ithaca."

That's the first she'd heard of two sisters. Come to think of it, Tessa had forgotten Ian had a brother until Brody showed up. She turned to Ian. "You have two sisters?"

"Bridget and Maeve, salt of the earth."

Brody made a disgusted noise. "They always gave me hell. He's the baby of the family. Everyone spoiled him."

Ian grinned from ear to ear. "Hey, I learned to work it. Either that, or the girls made me play tea party with them or dressed me up like some doll. I learned to stay on their good side." He nodded toward Brody. "Some people never figure things out. He battled them most of his life . . . and lost."

Brody chuckled—a deep, pleasant rumble. "Bridget can be a hellion if you cross her. She has red hair and the temper that goes with it." He narrowed his eyes at Tessa. "You seem awfully easy-going for a ginger."

"Ginger?" She frowned, and Brody laughed.

"But I could be wrong about that."

They yakked about homes and families for the rest of the meal, and Tessa enjoyed hearing about Ian's childhood. By the time they finished their desserts, David turned on the outside stereo and music pulsed in the air. People changed into their swimsuits, and the party moved to the pool.

"Get moving," Ian told Tessa. "Last one changed gets tossed in the water." He and Brody left the table.

"I think he'd do it," Keavin said. He hurried to find his suit.

Tessa shrugged. She didn't have the best figure in the world, but she didn't have the worst, either. Her only fussing point was her creamy skin that barely hinted at a tan, no matter how much time she spent in the sun. But what the heck? She slipped into Darinda's bedroom and came out in a modest black bikini.

When Ian spotted her walking toward them, he stopped talking in mid-sentence and stared. Brody followed his gaze and shook his head. "All that baking, and you don't have an ounce of fat. No wonder my brother spends so much time with you."

Tessa hurried to shake her head. "We're friends, nothing more."

"Then you're an honorable woman," Brody said, "because if you teased him, he'd be in trouble."

"I'm not Sadie. I'd never do that." The words came out sharper than she intended. She felt herself blush.

Brody studied her. "I see we each have a past. Yours hurt, too."

"It was a long time ago. I'm over it."

"The hell you are. Neither am I." Brody took her hand, and together, they jumped into the deep end of the pool.

When they surged out of the water, Tessa asked, "What happened to you?"

Ian cannonballed next to them, drowning them in his wake. Brody raked his hands through his thick black hair and said, "Married a woman who loved my money more than she loved me. I didn't see it until it was too late. I don't want Ian to make the mistake I did, to marry the wrong woman."

"Lily's not the wrong woman," Ian sputtered, shaking water from his face and hair as he joined them.

Brody shrugged massive shoulders. "We disagree. And stop shaking yourself off like that. You're like a wet dog running loose in the house."

Ian swam closer to Tessa. "Just because I'm the youngest in the family, Brody always thinks he's right."

"You can't hide behind your friend," Brody grumped. "I *am* right."

Tessa shook her head. "My brother's eight years older than I am, and he's the same way. Always giving me advice."

Brody smirked. "See? We learn by experience, and I have more experience."

"Not every woman marries for money," Ian protested.

Brody tread water. "You do have a lot of it, though. But that won't save you. Mine didn't save me. Lily likes bright lights and action. She's not going to last here."

"That's the perfect thing about it," Ian argued. "She travels all week long. By the time she comes here, she'll be ready to relax and spend time together."

"Doing what? How close is the nearest nightclub? Fancy restaurant? Has Lily spent a quiet night in front of a fireplace in her entire life?"

"She entertains clients or they entertain her all week. When she comes here, we have the lake and boating. Everything's at our fingertips."

"If you say so." If Brody's expression could grow more forbidding, it did. He looked at Tessa. "Do you like Lily?"

"She's always nice to me." A noncommittal answer, and that was all she was going to give. She knew better than to get in the middle of two brothers, especially these two. Both had dark hair. Both were good-looking enough to turn heads. One was charming. One was brooding. And she'd better be careful with both of them.

Darinda called from the middle of the pool, "You boys stop arguing among yourselves. Go mingle. I'm stealing Tessa. I want to hang with my buddy."

Ian pouted until David motioned for him and Brody to join the group of men, talking sports. "You're going to have to change allegiances now," he said. "We're all Colts fans. Baseball's up for grabs."

And the conversation took off.

When Tessa reached Darinda—hot and sexy in a yellow bikini—she glared. "How can you look that good after having two kids?"

"I married an Italian. Lots and lots of sex. It's great exercise."

Tessa rolled her eyes.

"Yeah, I gotcha, girl. I know what your problem is. You haven't had any for so long, you're drying up, and both of those brothers are hot."

"Stop it. Ian's taken, and Brody's so intense, he scares me."

"But there are good scares and bad," Darinda said, never dipping below her waistline, so that her cute, black curls still looked gorgeous. Tessa had jumped in the deep end and her hair was doing who-knows-what. "It's like watching those *Scream* movies," Darinda went on. "You scream 'Don't go in the basement,' but you know that actor won't listen to you. And it's not your fault he's gonna die. You tried to warn him, so it's all good. You WANT that thrill."

"This is my life," Tessa said, "not a movie."

"I'm just sayin', all thrills aren't bad."

"They're not all good either." Tessa leaned back against the edge of the pool and let the water buoy her body.

Darinda shrugged. "I don't think it matters. I think you're already smitten."

"Smitten?" Tessa stared at her.

"Too bad that cute Ian's already taken, because girl, you and him are like jam on toast."

Tessa didn't deny it. "But he *is* taken, and I know how it feels to be betrayed."

Darinda nodded. "History sucks. Experience can be worse than PMS."

Tessa bit her bottom lip. "I need to get some distance before I'm in trouble."

"Ain't gonna happen, friend. That's like trying to keep positive and negative magnets apart."

"I'm screwed, aren't I?"

Darinda gave a slow nod. "But I'll be here to help you pick up the pieces. This time, though, once you're done licking your wounds, you're not hiding again. You're gonna turn into a Valkyrie and go out to find your man."

Tessa laughed. "If you say so."

"I don't just say so, I'm gonna kick your ass if you duck and hide again."

How lucky was she to have such a good friend? "Agreed. I got it. I've been a weenie long enough."

Darinda's smile could light the world. It curled into a sign of happiness now. "Hallelujah! My girl's come back from the dead."

The rest of the party went remarkably well. By the time Tessa left to drive home, she was tired, but happy. Ian might break her heart, but she knew that ahead of time. It wasn't his fault or hers. And afterward, she'd learn from her mistakes. And this time, she'd be ready to move on.

Chapter 16

Tessa finished dicing the last of the parsley, capers, and anchovies to place in small glass canning jars. She seasoned the mix with salt, pepper, and a squeeze of lemon before topping them with extra virgin olive oil. Good. The Italian salsa verde was ready to go. She smiled at the jars lining the counters in the barn's kitchen. Red chili pepper sauce, tomato relish, and onion jam. She'd made enough to stock the barn's shelves for a month or so. A couple from the city had bought the last of them on Saturday and promised to return for more. There hadn't been any.

"We stopped here last fall and should have stocked up on these," the husband said. "We both have a thing for pasta."

Mondays were good days to work in the kitchen. The farm stand was open, but not the shop. This early in the spring, she had plenty of time to work between people stopping for salad fixings.

She was finishing up when Ian called. "I know you said I could bring Brody with me tonight, but we just finished all the work on the tennis courts. Want to come and try them out? You have a racket, so I'm thinking you must play."

"Give me an hour. I made chicken salad. Want me to bring it for sandwiches?"

"Brody loves chicken salad."

"You don't?"

"Not as much as Brody. Hope you made plenty."

When didn't she? She locked the barn and put a basket between the spinach and lettuces at the stand. People could grab what they needed and drop the money in the basket. Then she hurried to the house and changed clothes.

She smiled on the drive to Ian's place. A satisfied smugness hummed inside her. She'd grown up playing tennis. Had lots of private lessons. Ian thought he was going to play a girl so was guaranteed a win, but he had another think coming. She was damned good at the game.

She was surprised at the progress on the lodge when she pulled to the front door. The trim gleamed with new white paint. Wreathes of flowers hung on the red, double doors. The front lawn was edged and trimmed. Blooms spilled from flower boxes at the front windows of the three-story limestone house, and each wing displayed black shutters at the windows. *Damn, it looked good!*

Brody came to greet her when she parked her pickup by the front door. "Ian says you come bearing chicken salad."

"I kept it simple," she told him. "Added dill since it's for sandwiches."

"Works for me. I've never met a chicken salad I didn't like." He took the bag with the food from her and glanced inside. "A fruit salad, too? Another of my favorites."

"What can I say? You got lucky today." Brody's luck would end at the tennis courts. She followed him to the back patio. "The place looks great. Were you a part of that?"

He shrugged. Damn, the man had broad shoulders. "I work with a lot of landscapers in my business. I know what a difference presentation can make. We worked with your friend, Buck Krieger, at the nursery. He has nothing but good things to say about you."

She smiled. "Buck and I go back a long ways. I've known him since I spent summers with Grams and Gramps. He can be had with blueberry pies."

When they reached the back of the property, she noticed the new tennis courts and five, rental, log cabins beyond them. The cabins were bordered by the tennis courts on one side, the golf course—under construction across from them—and the lake. Not a bad setting.

"I talked Ian into buying ready-made cabins," Brody said. "Someday, if he wants to replace them with something fancier, he can, but people who like privacy might like them now."

She'd seen the log cabins for sale. Long and narrow, each had a small porch. They weren't spacious, but they were comfortable enough for sleeping quarters. Most people who came here would spend most of their time outdoors anyway.

They sat at the picnic table, overlooking the lake, while they ate. "What do you think of all the work we got done?" Ian asked.

"It's perfect. People should love it here."

When the ducks saw them, they headed in their direction. Tessa had brought extra bread for them, and Ian went to the shore to feed them.

"A little farther down," Brody called. "You want to keep them away from the pier and beach. Ducks can make a mess. No one wants to step in their droppings."

Ian blinked at him, surprised. "I hadn't thought of that."

"You don't fight Canada geese then. They're a nuisance on our lake back home."

When Ian finished his sandwich, he tugged at Tessa's hand. "Come on. Let's hit some balls. It's been a while since I've gotten to play."

Brody winced at his wording, but Tessa glanced at the four, immaculate courts on the far side of the yard. It was a perfect evening to play tennis. The air was cool. A slight breeze stirred the tree limbs. Her lips curved in a smile. "Did you finally buy a racket?"

"Better. I found the box that held my sports gear. I have my own." He reached for it and gave it a twirl.

Uh-oh, men who cherished their tennis rackets were usually pretty good at the game. She narrowed her eyes at him. Trouncing him might not prove as easy as she'd planned.

Brody grabbed two more sandwiches and a beer, then followed them to the tennis court. He settled himself on a comfortable park bench to watch.

"You're not going to play?" Tessa asked.

"No, this time, I'm going to enjoy watching."

"You can have first serve," Ian said.

She decided to start nice and solid, nothing too crazy. She'd gauge how well he played. She placed the ball in the center of his serve box, and he easily returned it—a nice, safe hit. She backhanded it to the other side of his court. He returned it to the base line of hers. They went back and forth, back and forth, each hit getting a little harder to return, with a little more power behind it. Finally, Ian hit a strong forehand shot, she rushed the net, and dropped the ball just over it on his side.

His mouth dropped open in surprise.

Her next serve hit the far corner of his box, and he had to work to return it . . . to her back line. She returned it to the center of his side, just inside his line, and he raced to get it. She smashed his return. He glared.

She aced her third serve, and Brody called, "Forty-love, bro! Get the lead out."

Ian's lips pressed into a tight line.

Tessa's first serve was out. Her second was safer, and Ian killed it.

Brody's voice took on a taunting tone. "Forty-fifteen. Kill him while you can, Tessa."

Things became brutal after that. Obviously, Ian didn't like to lose any more than she did. By the time they finished their set, sweat drenched each of them, and Ian had won after more deuces than Tessa could bear. It had been that close.

Brody watched them slump on the bench across from him and laughed. "Were you guys having fun out there?"

"It was great." Ian mopped his brow.

"I could wring you out like a dishrag." Brody tipped his beer bottle for another swig. "Maybe you two shouldn't play against each other."

Tessa took a deep breath, determined to be a good sport. "It's been months since I've been on a court. I enjoyed it."

"Sure you did." Brody sounded way too pleased with himself.

Ian reached to steal Brody's beer and made a face. "Uggh, I stink. I'm going to jump in the lake to cool off."

"Are you nuts?" Tessa stared. "It's the middle of May. The water's still cold."

He grimaced and looked at Brody. "Let's build an outdoor shower on the back of the house. It might come in handy. What do you think?"

"Not a bad idea. We'll check where the plumbing connects to the house."

Ian grinned. "When it's hot, I have the perfect solution. Come on, Tessa. I'll show you what I had done." He went to a tall tree whose branches reached out over the water. A new tire swing dangled from one of them. Ian grabbed the swing and motioned for Tessa to get in. "It's great. I'll give you a push. We had one of these when we were kids."

"So did I. Gramps strung it for me." She slid inside the oversized tire.

Ian pulled it back, then gave it a heave. The tire swung out over the water, the rope creaked, and then the knot came undone. Tessa flew farther, then plunged below the lake's surface. She sprang up, gasping, and swam for shore. When she hit solid footing, she ran toward Ian and Brody.

"Don't even think about it." Brody held up long arms to hold her away. "Ian's the stupid one who tried to freeze you to death."

Tessa changed direction and wrapped herself around Ian, pressing close for body warmth. Her teeth chattered, and her entire body shook.

"I'm sorry." Ian wrapped as much of himself around her as he could until his teeth chattered, too. "I'm *so* sorry." Even freezing, even dripping wet, Ian felt good.

"For God's sake!" Brody grabbed them both by their shirt collars and hauled them toward the house. Tessa's lightweight shirt clung to her, and she hugged herself to stay warm as she struggled to keep up with the McGregor brothers' long strides. Once inside the mudroom, Brody dumped them and went to fetch towels. Ian and Tessa shivered as water dripped off them onto the tile floor. He returned shortly with a big, bath towel for each of them.

They patted and dried, then wrapped themselves tight.

Ian looked at Tessa and grinned. "Damn, you're pretty when you're soaking wet."

Soaking wet was right. He'd nearly drowned her. She smacked his arm. "You're an idiot."

"That's what Brody tells me."

"And now you know why." Brody brought two, dry towels to replace their wet ones.

Bundled up, they went on the back patio to watch the sun set. Brody brought out a bottle of wine and three glasses, and they sipped in companionable silence.

Finally, Brody sighed. "Too bad I have to leave tomorrow. You two have kept me more entertained than I ever expected."

Tessa gave him a dirty look, and he laughed. "I'll miss you, Ginger."

She started to huff, and then smiled. "I'll miss you, too. The next time you come to visit Ian, make sure you stop in to see me."

He frowned. "That'll be an automatic. You feed him every day."

The sun sank low to the water, staining it rosy pink. Was there anything more glorious than a sunset? Tessa shrugged. "Feeding Ian's only temporary. When Lily moves here, everything will change."

"Oh, yeah, I forgot. Maybe I'll stay at your place and stop in to visit the lodge."

"Not fair," Ian protested. "Eventually, you and Lily will learn to like each other."

"Hmm." Brody glanced at Tessa. "You have an extra room, don't you?"

She laughed. "I do, but we'll see what happens. You like your brother."

A smile lifted Brody's wide lips. "Problem solved, I'll come from Monday through Friday. Lily will be on a trip somewhere."

Ian scowled, but Tessa wondered if that might not work better. She doubted Brody changed his mind easily once he formed an opinion.

Brody surprised her by reaching for her hand. His grip was warm and firm. A woman would feel secure if Brody held her. "It's been a pleasure getting to know you, Tessa Lawrence. I hope you stay a part of my life."

Tears threatened. A lump caught in her throat. She stood and reached to hug him. Long, strong arms pulled her close, and she smiled. When she straightened to call it a night and leave, she caught Ian's expression—troubled.

What now? He should be happy her brother got along so well with her. She ignored his mood and said, "Have a safe trip home, Brody." When he started to rise, she waved him back into his seat. "Don't get up. No need to. You two enjoy your time together before you have to go."

She circled the house and started her pickup. If she flirted with Brody, would he be interested? She didn't think so. But they could be lifelong friends, just like Keavin and her.

Chapter 17

Tuesday blistered with unseasonable heat. Tessa woke feeling sticky and warm. After her shower, she pulled her long hair into a high ponytail to get it off her neck. It dried kinky from too much humidity. According to the weatherman, the heat would build during the day, then a thunderstorm would blow it away in the early evening. Indiana weather. Always changeable.

She carried her morning coffee outside and wrinkled her nose. Too hot and muggy to work in the gardens. Maybe a good thing. Before the weather was truly miserable, she picked greens and herbs for the farm stand and left them with the donations basket. If anyone needed something else, she left a sign to stop by the house. Her house— she frowned at the thin layer of dust on every surface. It needed a good clean. She'd been putting it off. She cranked on the air conditioner, grabbed the dust mop, and got busy. By late afternoon, she felt drained from all the sweeping, mopping, and scrubbing, but the old place gleamed.

Sweat trickled down her back and soaked her bra. It pooled in her cleavage. Disgusting. She turned to head to the shower when a car pulled into her drive. Hmm, maybe the greens had sold out. She could always pick more. She swiped her arm across her shiny forehead and went to greet her visitor. Then froze.

The car parked in her drive belonged to her parents. According to Grams, they weren't visiting until next month, or maybe later. Her mother rushed across the lawn to hug her, stopped and sniffed, then shook her head. "You're a mess."

Tessa smiled. "I love you, too. I just finished cleaning the house from top to bottom. I took a shower this morning, but it's too humid."

Her dad didn't mind. He crushed her to him. "Hey Copperhead, good to see you!"

Her brother came up behind him, grinning. "I see you haven't changed."

"Give me a break. I didn't know you were coming."

"That's my fault," her mom said. "I decided it would be better to travel in spring, when it wasn't so hot. Maybe we'll hit the cherry blossoms and spring gardens on the east coast."

"It's too late for that," Craig said. Her brother had probably looked it up on the Internet. He was always organized. Unlike her mother. Mom might sit on every board for every club she belonged to, but no one was silly enough to make her the head of anything. They relied on her energy and enthusiasm instead. And connections. Mom had lots of connections.

Her dad wrapped an arm around Tessa's shoulders and started into the house. "The place is as pretty as ever."

"I'd better call Mom," her mother said. "If your grandmother misses anything, she'll have my head."

As usual, they settled in the kitchen. Tessa put pitchers of lemonade and iced tea on the table, along with glasses, and everyone helped themselves. "How long can you stay?"

"Only two days and nights." Craig's voice was dry. "Mom's on a mission. We're going to see more sites than anyone should bother with in one week."

"Where's Nora?" Tessa liked Craig's lawyer-wife. She was perfect for Craig—strong enough to speak her mind and fun enough to enjoy every minute with him.

"Couldn't come. Working on a big case right now. We're going to Michigan in late July, renting a boat. You should come up to visit us."

She shook her head. "That's my busy time. Maybe I can meet you somewhere in January or February."

"That would be fun. Maybe some place hot, like Key West."

Mom slid her cell back in her pocket and reached for the lemonade. "You two, always plotting together. I want to catch up on all the gossip. Time to spill your guts, kid."

Tessa shook her head. "You have such high hopes. You know how boring I am."

"That's not what I've heard." Her mother's grin looked naughty. "Grams says you've met a hot guy."

"Yup, my neighbor, the one who's engaged. You'll meet him tonight. He's coming for supper."

"About that, you're not cooking." Mom's tone was final. "We surprised you, so we're taking you out to eat. Your friend's invited, too."

A good thing. Tessa had two ribeyes to grill. Not enough to go around. "I'll call Ian and warn him that family's here. It's his choice if he braves that."

"I'd like to meet him." Her brother's expression turned serious. "Grams said you get along really well."

"He's a neighbor. I even got along with Sam Dramer. I softened him up with jams and jellies. It's easier. No border disputes."

Her dad grinned. "Nice try, but it's more than that. Grams said you two just clicked. I'd like to meet him, too. A guy finally made you think all men weren't the enemy. You'll see us in a new light."

She felt her shoulders relax. Good, they understood. "He's genuinely nice, and he's totally in love with Lily. I like that about him."

"And it makes you feel safe." Craig studied her. "You can be yourself with him, because he's taken."

"That, too." Tessa stood. "Want some help carrying your stuff upstairs so you can get settled?"

Her mom pursed her lips. "Are there clean sheets on the beds?"

"Yup, no one's used them that I know of. I'm glad I cleaned today. You guys could have died of dust allergies."

They trounced to the car and carried suitcases up the steps. Craig took the room that faced the front, and her parents the bigger one that looked out over the lake. A bathroom separated them.

Her mom looked around and smiled. "It looks better without my old posters covering the walls. I had a happy childhood here."

Just then, the doorbell rang, and Grams' voice called, "Hey, where's my long-lost daughter?"

Mom ran down the stairs to greet her. The rest of them followed. They moved to the screened porch at the back of the house and spent the next two hours catching up. Finally, Mom frowned at Tessa and said, "If we're going out tonight, you need to get ready. I'll help you pick out something nice to wear."

"I've been dressing myself for a while now, Mom."

Her mother—trim and fit at sixty, with light-brown hair and green eyes—grimaced. "I can tell. You don't use the sunblock and beauty products I send you, do you? Look at your freckles! Look at that hair. Do you use products for the frizz?"

Grams laughed. "Uh-oh, you've been busted, Kid. Better move it and try to look decent."

Her mother turned to Grams. "She's not the only one busted. What about you? I've heard rumors about you lately."

"About me?" Grams tried to look innocent. "I thought we were trying to keep things pleasant. Who ratted?"

"Hazel Newsome, we still Facebook each other."

"Damn that Hazel. I let her have sleepovers with you whenever she wanted to."

Tessa smiled and started toward her room.

"Sure, leave an old lady alone to defend herself," Grams called. "You know your mom can turn into the inquisitor from Hell."

Tessa laughed and headed to the shower. "Nothing I say is going to save you."

Twenty minutes later, her mom knocked on the door, saw Tessa bundled in her bathrobe, and slid inside her bedroom. She shook her head when Tessa held up the same flowered skirt she'd worn when Ian took her out to eat.

"Nope, we're eating in town, probably at the diner, but I still want you to look nice." She started flipping through the clothes in Tessa's closet. "Here." She tossed a pair of hip-hugging khaki pants on the bed. A snug-fitting black V-neck shirt followed them. She turned her head while Tessa tugged them on, then nodded approval. "You can actually see your figure now. You usually hide it under baggy tees."

Next, she looked through Tessa's makeup drawer. She pulled out the many under-used products she'd sent her. "This." Brown eyeliner. "And this." Bronze eyeshadow. She chose a foundation and blush, lip gloss, and perfume. Then she pulled Tessa's hair up in a high, messy bun with strands falling to frame her face.

When Tessa looked in the mirror, she had to admit her mom had a knack. The reflection that gazed back at her didn't look half bad.

By the time they rejoined the others on the porch, Ian sat with them. At Tessa's frown, Craig said, "I saw him drive up. Cute, little car. Going to be interesting to see how it survives on these roads in the winter. Anyway, I invited him in."

Tessa turned to introduce her mom to him, but Ian's gaze stayed riveted on her. He looked bemused. She sighed. "Snap out of it. Ian, this is my mother, Connie. Mom, this is Ian, my next door neighbor."

"Ian's invited us over to see what he's done to Sam's old place," Tessa's dad said. "He's turning it into a lodge."

Her mom's face lit up. "How wonderful! I'd love to see it."

"It's not as nice as this." Ian motioned to Tessa's house. "But Tessa helped me pick out things, and it turned out looking comfortable and homey."

Grams rode over with Tessa's family, leaving Tessa to ride with Ian.

"You look nice." Ian looked her up and down with appreciation.

"So do you." Ian always looked good. Dressed in expensive jeans, like Craig's, and a polo shirt, he fit the part of dressy casual. Of course, Ian looked good no matter what he had on . . . or off.

"Your family seems nice."

"They're great." Tessa smiled. "They love to give me grief, but I've always felt loved. I'm more like Dad, pretty laid-back. Craig takes after Mom. They both love to be on the go, in the middle of everything."

They parked near the front door and waited for her dad to pull up behind them. Then Ian motioned them inside. "Welcome to Lakeview Stables."

Mom's gaze swept the property, and she let out a long breath. "I'm impressed. When you're finished, you can offer guests a little bit of everything."

Ian grinned. "No mountains for skiing, but I'll have tennis, golf, horseback riding, and the lake. The golf course won't be finished till next spring, though."

"And gourmet food." Craig nodded when Ian turned to him, surprised. "This area has hit some of the travel magazines because of its specialty items."

"I have topnotch suppliers lined up," Ian told him. "And I've hired a chef to keep the guests satisfied."

That was the first Tessa had heard about the chef. She hadn't thought about who'd cook the meals here.

"A name we'd know?" Craig asked.

"I doubt it, but she's worked in a few trendy restaurants. Paula's all into the farm-to-table movement." Ian glanced at his watch. "I'd better show you around before Tessa starts gnawing on us. She hates late suppers."

When Tessa scowled, Grams laughed. "Give the girl a little pity. It's a long time between lunch and supper when you work summer hours at the stand."

Ian gave them the grand tour. It was the first time Tessa saw the finished guest rooms, and Ian's gaze locked with hers. When she smiled her approval, he looked relieved.

As they finished up, back at the big, double doors, Tessa's dad shook his head. "I'd have never thought anyone could do so much with this old place. Good luck to you, son."

Ian's color heightened at the term, and Craig's eyes narrowed. He glanced at Tessa. She shrugged. It was odd the things that pleased Ian.

They divided up again for the drive into town, and when they settled in the diner, other people moseyed by their table to yak.

"Long time no see," old acquaintances told Mom and Dad.

The meal took longer than it should have, with bygone friends stopping often to talk. Tessa only half-listened. With six people crowded around a rectangular table, it was close quarters. Her thigh jostled against Ian's. Did he realize their legs were touching? He didn't show it. Should she reposition herself, or would that draw his attention? Would Ian wonder why she hadn't moved before? The heat of his skin sizzled through the fabric of his jeans and her khakis. What would it feel like to have her bare legs twined with his? She took a long drink of iced water. What was wrong with her? Hormone overload.

By the time they left the restaurant, it was getting late, and her libido was in overdrive.

"I'll drop Tessa off at her place, then head back to the lodge," Ian told them. "I have a big day tomorrow. Have to drive to the city to set up some advertising. I'm ready to open my doors."

"You won't be at supper tomorrow night?" Craig asked.

Ian shook his head. "It was nice meeting all of you, though. No wonder Tessa's turned out so great. She came from good stock."

Tessa practically hugged the passenger door on the drive home. One more accidental touch, and her reputation might go down the tubes. Her fingers itched to clamp his thigh, work their way higher. How embarrassing would that be—to be banned from Ian's house so that she couldn't ravish him?

When they pulled in front of her bungalow, she sighed her relief. Her parents pulled in behind them. She turned to Ian to thank him for the ride home and looked away quickly. A smile pulled at her lips. She hadn't been the only one struggling with inappropriate feelings. A bulge poked at his jeans. She tossed him a smile and hurried to open her own door. If he reached across her to help, they'd be having sex on the front seat.

Craig came and wrapped an arm around Tessa's shoulder to wave Ian off. Once he was out of sight, he gave her a quick squeeze. "That guy thinks you walk on water. It's a good thing we didn't tell him all the horror stories of your youth."

She took a deep breath. She needed to center herself. Hopefully, no one noticed the chemistry sizzling between them. "What horror stories? You were hardly ever around."

"I'm eight years older than you. Who wants a tagalong ruining their fun? But I was always there when you needed me. Still am. Remember that."

She blinked at him. "Ian and I are only neighbors. We're friends."

"Yeah, keep telling yourself that, and when his Lily moves in, if you need some time away from here, Nora and I will whisk you off somewhere."

Okay, so he'd noticed. Tears stung her eyes. "You're a keeper of a brother. You know that, right?"

"It's mutual, sis. We don't have much in common, and maybe that's why I like you so much."

They went in the house to be with their parents and Grams. Her pulse quit beating too fast. Her nerves relaxed back to normal. The rest of the night passed with memories and laughter. Tessa might want to sell her family at times, but she couldn't live without them.

Chapter 18

The one whole day Tessa had with her family flew by too fast. When they woke on Thursday morning, they started loading suitcases into Dad's car.

"We only stopped here to see you," Mom said. "We know your schedule. Thursdays, you bake all day, so it's a good time for us to leave."

"That, and *you* have reservations at a hotel seven hours away." Craig looked at his watch and sighed. "Mom's always been a woman with an agenda."

Grams came to wave them off and then she and Tessa walked to the barn together. Neither of them joked or laughed much as they worked. Goodbyes left an aura of disquiet for a few days before routine settled in once more. Tessa loved seeing her family, but always missed them for a while after they left.

They finished faster than usual and Grams hurried to her car.

"Let me guess," Tessa called. "Is Miguel bringing supper tonight?"

Grams nodded. "See you in the morning!" And off she went.

Tessa finished filling the glass cases with cakes and pies, then locked the barn and headed toward the lake. She was staring out across its deep blue waters when her cell phone rang. She looked at the caller I.D.—Ian.

"Hey, I just saw Grams' car fly past my place. Can I come over early? I've got an idea I'd like to throw at you."

Her breath caught, and she chided herself. She pushed her fantasies back where they belonged—buried. "Sure, I've got brats and sauerkraut in the Crock-Pot. We can eat any time."

"See you in a few minutes then!" Ian hung up.

Tessa shook her head. She had to get a grip. Any little nuance with Ian and her mind took her to places she shouldn't go. She was in the kitchen, digging buns and potato chips out of the pantry, when Ian gave a quick knock at the door and hurried in.

He reminded her of a kid at Christmas, all ready to tear wrapping paper off presents.

He started talking before he reached the kitchen. "The inn's in pretty good shape. The guest rooms and the cabins are finished and furnished. The tennis courts are ready to go. What if I invited the town to an open house on Sunday so that people can see it before I open it for business? I know this is last minute, spur of the moment, but it could be fun, couldn't it?"

Tessa blinked. That was the last thing she'd expected him to say, but once she thought about it, she liked the idea. "If you're really serious, you should call Grams. You're not giving people much notice, but that's all right. We're not a formal town. She'll spread the word before anyone goes to bed tonight. And the town's rooting for you. They'll show up, and they'll like seeing what you've done."

He couldn't stand still. He bounced on the balls of his feet. "What do I need to do? I should have food of some kind. Drinks? I want to do this right."

"Has your chef come yet?" Tessa asked.

"No, the wing she's going to live in is ready for her, but she has to wait for her kids to get out of school before they move here."

"Kids?"

"She's a single mom."

Wow. Ian was taking on a lot, but he seemed fine with it. She thought a minute. "In that case, I'd keep the food simple, but elegant."

"Like what?"

They made a list—crab spread on crostini, shrimp and fresh pineapple kebabs wrapped in bacon, beef tenderloin sliders, and roasted asparagus.

"Who should I hire to make all this? Does anyone do catering in Mill Pond?" he asked.

"Yeah, me, but I can't manage this much on my own. You'll have to come to help me."

Ian frowned. "Do I need to worry about vegetarians?"

They added a white bean puree on crostini, too. She could make the puree a day ahead.

He nodded, satisfied, and Tessa began to get excited about the get-together. All of their friends would be there. It would be an event. Then he ruined it. "Lily will love this," he said.

Lily. The girl who showed up, all bright and sparkly, after everyone else did all the work. Tessa—the drudge, who *did* all the work. She bit her bottom lip.

Ian noticed. "Lily's coming tomorrow night. I meant to take her into the city, but I thought of this instead. She loves being a hostess. Maybe it will get her excited about the resort."

Maybe. *When pigs fly.* Tessa was beginning to wonder. "Mill Pond's a great place to hang out. You should take her to the vineyard on the east side of the lake tomorrow night. It's offering wine and cheese tastings. There's even going to be live jazz."

"Lily would like that, and then you and I can work together on Saturday and Sunday to get everything ready."

Oh, goody, should she cheer now or later? She swallowed her bad humor. She wanted this to be a success for him. "People around here really like you, not just for business, but as a person."

"I like them, too. You know, I've spent my whole life trying to be decent to people. In finance, sometimes I had to work at it. I don't have to here. You guys are solid."

"So you've always been an upstanding kind of guy?"

"I try. Brody swears I was a brat as a kid, though."

"Did you break a friend's crayon in first grade?"

He smiled. "Back then, I'm sure I did worse, probably pulled a girl's pigtail and she never forgot."

Tessa laughed. "If that's the worst you did, you're in pretty good shape."

"Yeah, I'm not much of a rebel."

No, he was everything wonderful. And that was the problem. Tessa shook her head. "Well, if we have everything planned for your open house, let's eat supper and call it a night. I work in the bakery tomorrow, and you're going to have a busy weekend."

He seemed reluctant to change mode, but pushed to his feet to grab paper plates and silverware. "You're right. I've got plenty of things to keep me busy tomorrow. The golf carts I ordered are coming, and I want to pick up the brochures I ordered, so that I can hand them out on Sunday."

She frowned. "But the golf course won't be finished till next year, right?"

"Right, but the carts will be nice for people to take in the sights." He hesitated. "Thanks for helping me . . . again. You're the best."

"That's what—"

"Neighbors do," he finished for her, then grinned. "I'm starving. Let's eat."

He left the minute they finished their meal. She'd work in the bakery tomorrow, then eat supper, alone. On a Friday night. Which never used to bother her. But Ian would be with Lily, damn it.

Chapter 19

Friday brought a flood of customers. Grams and Tessa could hardly keep up, and when the last person walked out the barn door, they sagged with relief. Thank goodness Kayla had the day off school and was manning the farm stand. They sold out of greens, spring peas, and asparagus.

Grams shook her head, bemused. "Well, it's a good thing we kept pies and cakes in the back cooler for tomorrow."

Tessa noticed that lately, Grams was ready to leave earlier and earlier. She tired faster, and Miguel was bringing suppers to her place more and more often. Grams always offered to stay and help finish up, but Tessa could tell she was worn out. "Call it quits," she told her. "I'll load the cases for tomorrow and clean up. It won't take me that long."

With a grateful smile, Grams headed toward the door.

Kayla came in with the money from the produce stand and stalled around. Tessa studied her. "Is everything all right?"

The girl looked uncomfortable. Maybe she didn't like her new job. Maybe she worried about quitting when she and Luther lived in the log cabin. Finally, she took a deep breath and said, "Luther's mowing at Ian's place, so he'll be working later than usual. I was wondering if you'd like me to stay and help you with anything."

Tessa blinked. All that agony over extra hours? But Kayla still didn't feel comfortable around her. Tessa wasn't sure if she felt at ease around anyone but Luther, so she started with something simple. "You never told me why you didn't have school today."

"Oh, that. It was our senior field trip. The school hired buses to drive us to Cedar Point to go on all of the rides."

"And you didn't go?"

Kayla grimaced. "I was worried the rides would make me sick." She rested a hand on her stomach. Her pregnancy didn't show yet, but that didn't mean she'd feel good after too many roller coasters.

Tessa kept busy sweeping. If she didn't look at Kayla, the girl didn't get as nervous. "When's your last day of school?"

"On Tuesday, we go half a day."

"I can't believe May's almost over." Where had the time gone? Tessa had gotten everything done that needed done, but it had felt rushed this year.

Kayla hesitated. "Do you still want me to work, full-time, like Luther used to during the summer?"

"If you feel up to it. He's probably told you what he does and how, right? And I gave you a copy of the schedule we usually use."

"He says he usually got everything done in three or four hours a day during the week. I like to keep busy." Her gaze dipped to the floor. She couldn't meet Tessa's eyes. "My aunt used to let me help her bake pies. Said I was pretty good at it—if you ever need help in the kitchen, I mean."

"Really?" Tessa glanced at the empty glass cases. The bakery was selling more pies and cakes than ever. "For right now, why don't you help me fill these up again? Grams and I baked extra yesterday. We can talk while we work." It was amazing what she and Grams could get done when they were both in a no-nonsense mood.

It was nice, having an extra pair of hands. She and Kayla worked well together, and in half an hour, the cases were filled and the shop was cleaned. Kayla stopped in the kitchen to look at the list of specials taped to a cupboard door. Reading down week after week of sale items, she widened her eyes in surprise. "I don't know how to make all of these. My aunt only taught me a few cakes and pies."

"The recipes aren't hard. I can teach them to you. When Ian opens his lodge, he wants me to supply the desserts. Grams doesn't want to come any more than she does, and I can't do it all myself. What if you work a couple of hours Monday through Wednesday mornings?"

Kayla lit up, and Tessa was amazed. The girl looked tired and washed-out until she got excited, and then she had a glow about her. No wonder Luther had fallen for her. That boy needed some sparkle in his life. "I'm not book smart," Kayla told her, "but I'm a fast learner on things I can do with my hands. If you teach me, I'll try hard to learn."

Tessa swallowed a lump in her throat. Damn, she was as big of a softie as Grams. "That's all I can ask, but pregnant women get tired, don't they? I heard they need naps in the afternoons."

"It's been hard not to fall asleep in school, but if I'm up and moving, I'm all right."

"If the baking gets to be too much for you, let me know, and we'll figure out something else."

Kayla glanced at the lists again. "I always wanted to own a tea shop and bake fancy little desserts and make finger sandwiches."

Tessa blinked. "That would be a great idea for Ian's lodge. Mind if I mention that to him? Instead of lunch, he could offer afternoon teas."

Kayla's eyes lit with excitement. "Do you think he'd like that?"

"Why wouldn't he? It would be something unique and special he could offer guests."

"We could come up with all kinds of tea cakes and tiny éclairs."

Tessa laughed. "You've thought about this."

A blush colored Kayla's neck and cheeks. "I've read every Agatha Christie novel there is. When Miss Marple had afternoon tea, it always sounded so romantic."

"You're right. It does."

"Do you have things we could make for it?"

"I have lots of ideas, but if you sell our secret recipes, I'll have to steal your first-born child."

Kayla stared, then noticed the wry smile that pulled at Tessa's lips, and she broke into giggles. "I won't tell. I promise."

"Then we're good. Want to start training on Wednesday? You'll be out of school, and Ian's about ready to open for business."

With a quick nod, Kayla started for the door, then turned around and hurried back. She wrapped Tessa in a brief hug. "You've been awfully good to Luther and me. Thank you."

"Get out of here," Tessa growled. Lord, the girl was going to bring her to tears. "We're going to be even busier tomorrow. Be ready."

When the door shut behind her, Tessa let out a long sigh. Somehow, lately, her nice, quiet life had gotten more complicated. Caring about people came with a price tag. But she did care about Luther and Kayla, so there was no point in fussing about it.

She locked up and started for the house. Sweat trickled down her back and rimmed her hairline before she reached the white, picket fence that circled the small, back yard. What had happened to their cooler temperatures? The heat had risen, and so had the humidity. She opened the back gate to enter the yard when she heard an odd noise.

She stopped to listen, but she must have been mistaken. Everything was quiet. She started to the house again. Something bleated. *A bleat?* Her neighbor, Evan Meyers, raised goats. Had one wandered off?

She started to the berry patches, where she thought the sound came from. She stopped, short, when she saw a sheep, lying on its side, crying out in pain. Oh, lord, was it dying? She knew Bob Thornton raised a small flock of sheep, along with his alpacas. The sheep, he used for wool, and the lambs . . . well, people loved the taste of them. She pulled her cell from her jeans pocket and dialed Bob's number.

"A sheep's lying by my berry patch, and I think it's in trouble. Is it one of yours?"

"I'll be there in five minutes," Bob said.

The sheep's bleat was louder this time. The poor thing sounded desperate. If it was dying, it shouldn't die alone. Tessa went to kneel beside it and stroked its fuzzy head. The sheep cried out again, and she wrapped her arms around its neck to soothe it. The sheep pressed its face against her thigh, panting with pain. Then it raised its face slightly, thrashed, and two, gangly legs appeared near its rear.

Tessa shut her eyes. *No, no, no.* This couldn't be happening. She looked to the heavens. Her grandparents had raised chickens once upon a time, but their babies broke through the shells of eggs. This was totally disgusting, and she had no idea how to help the mother or the lamb.

A truck came to a quick stop in her driveway, and she called, "Over here. Hurry!"

In minutes, Bob knelt behind the sheep, grabbed the legs, and when the mother sheep pushed again, he pulled. It took a couple of tries, but soon, a baby lamb stood on wobbly legs and nuzzled its mother.

Bob and Tessa walked to the outside hose to wash up. Bob sighed. "That sheep's lucky you found her. The lamb came breech. They might not have made it, either of them."

Tessa felt slightly nauseous. She was a country girl, yes. But she didn't raise any livestock, and now, she was grateful.

Bob looked at her and smiled. "This is one of my smartest sheep. She must have noticed that no lambs reach a ripe age on our farm. I think she came here to give her baby a future."

Tessa started to shake her head. "Nope, I don't want a sheep. I'm too busy to care for animals."

"Doesn't matter," Bob said. "I like this girl's gumption. That newborn lady is going to stick around. We'll raise her and keep her for her wool."

Relief unwound in Tessa's belly. She could feel her nerves relax.

Bob smiled. "We'll name her Tessie, after you. Maybe Ester will stain her wool a copper color."

Tessa laughed. "Not sure that would catch on, so if Ester isn't hot on the idea, I understand." She looked at the lamb. "Be nice to her."

"As your namesake? The kid's got it made."

She helped Bob load mother and baby in the back of his pickup and then waved them away. She'd almost made it to the house when her cell rang again. Maybe Ester, calling about the new lamb. "Yes?"

It took her a minute to recognize Lily's voice. "Tessa? I'm so excited about Sunday's open house. Did your grandmother tell everyone about it?"

"The news is all over town. That's all most of my customers talked about this morning."

"Is there a way we could have music, too? Do you know any good bands we could hire?"

Tessa hesitated. "This is a late afternoon event, two to four. Most of the townspeople will come, eat and visit for a while, then leave. They won't stay long enough to dance."

A sigh greeted that. Lily said, "What will people wear? Should I dress up?"

"It's warm enough for sundresses or khakis with fun tops. Mill Pond doesn't get too glamorous."

Another sigh. "Well, thanks, and thanks for everything you're doing to help Ian."

"No problem." But Tessa could tell the open house didn't meet Lily's expectations. Tessa didn't know what kinds of events Lily usually attended, but they were obviously more exciting than this. She fretted for a minute, then pushed her worries aside. Once Lily got to know the people in Mill Pond, once she connected with them, she'd realize what a wonderful location Ian had chosen. She'd be happy here. Ian was taking her to the winery tonight for the wine and cheese tasting. There'd be jazz. Lily would see why tourists loved coming here.

Chapter 20

The bakery was slammed on Saturday. Beautiful weather brought tourists from other towns, and the traffic on the county road buzzed with extra activity. Tessa smiled and chatted to each customer who came and went, but Ian stayed in the back of her thoughts. They were friends, and she didn't want to risk that, but she needed to find a way to pull away from him. She shouldn't have worried. Close to the end of the day, Lily stopped in to ask if Tessa had any frozen coffee cakes for sale.

As usual, Lily couldn't look any cuter. Short-shorts showed off her shapely legs. A deep V-neck displayed her cleavage. A high ponytail bobbed at the back of her head, and make-up rimmed her blue eyes, making them look huge. How did she do it? How did she always look sparkly and feminine?

She grinned at Tessa. "All that damn boyfriend of mine talks about is your bakery, so I thought I'd better come to see it for myself. Ian told me while I'm here, I might as well pick up something for breakfast. I might stay over a couple of days, so I need pastries for Monday and Tuesday, too."

"I don't have a streusel," Tessa said, "but I have cinnamon rolls. I'll go dig some out of the freezer for you."

Grams came to the counter to make small talk while Tessa went to search for the rolls. Tessa heard Grams say, "So, did you like the winery? The owners give tours in the summer."

Lily answered, "It was all right, sort of quiet, but Ian got out the previous owner's pontoon and took me on a boat ride this morning. The lake's beautiful. I'm trying to talk him into buying jet skis and hiring bands on weekends. Then we could party more."

"The winery has a band every Friday in the summer," Tessa heard Grams say.

"But it's jazz, and the locals sit around and visit with each other. Kind of dead. I'm talking about dance music."

"The bar has dance music." Grams was being persistent. To her, no place could compare to Mill Pond.

"We've been there. I've met the locals." Lily let it stand at that.

Grams gave her a look as Tessa hurried to the counter to ring up Lily's order. When Lily gave a cheerful wave and left, Grams huffed out a sigh. "That girl's a spoiled, little snot."

Tessa shrugged. "She's used to big cities. She likes the night scene. It's going to take her a while to adjust."

"Not gonna happen." Grams started for the door. "Well, it's been fun and all, kid, but my bunions need a rest. Don't worry about fixing me supper tomorrow night. Miguel—"

"—is bringing you something." Tessa smiled. "I never thought you'd ditch me for a guy."

"Such an innocent," Grams told her. "But I'll still see you three times a week in the bakery."

Tessa froze and stared. Was Grams saying that their Sunday nights were a thing of the past? It sure sounded like it. "Wait a minute. Are you talking about *every* Sunday?"

Grams put her hands on her hips. "It's time you found new people to hang out with. It's time we both move on."

What the hell? Tessa fussed under her breath as she cleaned and locked up. When she went to check on Kayla, the girl was almost finished, too.

"Sorry I didn't get in to help you," Kayla said, "but we sold out of everything—twice. I had to put out the money basket to go pick more."

"It's like that once it gets warm and there are more products to offer."

Kayla glanced at her watch, but waited politely.

"I'm finished here," Tessa told her. "I'll see you on Wednesday for baking lessons."

Kayla grinned and took off. Luther must be at the cabin, waiting for her.

As Tessa trudged to the house, she sighed. She'd always looked forward to seeing Grandma on Sunday nights. Was that a bad thing? How sad was it when your grandma hinted that your social life was pathetic? She'd never felt lonely before, but suddenly, eating suppers, alone, in front of the TV didn't appeal to her.

No worries tonight. Tessa heated up leftovers and took a short break before Ian dropped in. Right away, they got started on making food for the open house. The bean puree was simple, and they finished it in no time. But Ian had called last night and asked if maybe they could have some small, easy desserts, too. Tessa had thought about that herself. Every gathering needed a sweet treat at the end. She decided to make pudding shooters in short, champagne-type glasses.

"What *is* a shooter?" Ian asked.

Tessa placed heavy saucepans on the stove. "I was going to make two different kinds—lemon and chocolate. You put pudding in the bottom of the glass, then whipped cream, then crumbled cookies, then another layer of each. We can make the pudding today and fill the glasses tomorrow."

He licked his lips, ready to start.

Tessa hated to bring it up, but said, "Why don't you call Lily and see if she'd like to pitch in? I meant to invite her, but forgot."

"Not her thing. I'm not sure if she's ever touched a stove." He shrugged. "She promised to give the resort a try, but she wasn't ready for how hard start-up would be. She's not happy I left her tonight, so I decided to give her a special surprise. I invited some of her friends from work to spend the weekend with us, so they'll be here for the open house, too."

Tessa stared. "I was hoping Lily would get to know the people around here better." That wouldn't happen if she had friends around her.

Ian squared his shoulders. "I know Mill Pond is an adjustment for her. I'd like to make it as easy as possible."

Tessa didn't say anything, deciding silence was sometimes the better part of valor.

"Once she plugs in here, she'll feel better about this place."

Tessa wasn't so sure about that. She wondered if part of Lily wanted Ian to fail, so that he'd move back to New York.

Ian sighed. "Anything worthwhile gives you gray hairs, right? I knew that coming into this. I love this place. I love . . ." He faltered to a halt. "I don't know what I'd do if I had to give up and go back to my old life. Lily wants to settle on the West Coast once we get this place going. I wouldn't even be close to my family."

Before Tessa could say anything, a small caravan of cars drove past the bungalow.

"Come on. I want you to meet them, and then we can come back and finish up." Ian waved her to the golf cart he'd driven, and they zipped down the road. He pulled in behind his guests, and amid the honking of horns and laughter, Lily hurried out of the lodge. She was dressed in a designer top that scooped low enough to be revealing with a snug fit to accent her small waistline. Her jeans were skintight. She looked adorable, as usual. When she saw her friends, her face broke into a smile. She ran to Ian and hugged him.

"I should have known you'd make this weekend wonderful. You always do. I love you, babe." She stood on tiptoe to brush a kiss across his lips, then ran to greet her friends.

Ian grimaced. He turned to Tessa. "After we finish the desserts, I'm treating everyone to drinks at our local bar. There's a band, right?"

"Yup, Chase hires someone every Friday and Saturday." And this time, Lily wouldn't have to rub shoulders with the *locals*. She could mingle with her buddies.

He grinned, but the sparkle didn't reach his eyes. "This will be a good test run for the resort. Bet it gives me lots of ideas for when I open the doors." He hesitated. "Tess, thanks again. Thanks for being there for me."

"We're neighbors."

"No, we're friends. You're the best. I wish Lily . . ." He let it drop. "Anyway, thanks."

She forced a smile. Did it look as pathetic as his? "Look, just take me home and drop me off. I can whip out the puddings in no time. You need to knock this out of the park. Have fun with Lily."

"Right." He drove her home, sat for a minute to watch her walk inside, then put on his best host face and went to join Lily.

Ian had never called her *Tess* before. They were spending too much time together, getting too close. The attraction pulled too strong. She needed to give herself more space, remove herself from temptation.

Chapter 21

Ian walked in the barn at nine a.m. on Sunday. He looked like crap. Okay, not true. Even with bed head and stubble, dressed in old jeans and a rumpled T-shirt, he was gorgeous, maybe even sexier. Tessa had to force her fingers not to reach out and stroke his jaw, but his eyes had dark circles under them, and he hardly had enough energy to move.

Tessa was no ball of energy herself. She grinned at him. "Did you brush your teeth?"

"Had to." He ran his tongue over them. "My breath smelled like stale beer."

Lovely. She put the beef tenderloins on the counter to come to room temperature. "You must have had a good time last night."

He grimaced. "Lily promised we'd leave Chase's at midnight since we had so much work to do today. I should have known better. She and her friends didn't quit dancing till the bar closed at two."

"Is everything set up at your place? You won't have time to cook and get tables and plates ready."

He sighed. "Everyone was still asleep when I left, but Lily promised they'd all pitch in and get that part finished for me."

Another promise. Maybe she'd keep this one. Not Tessa's problem.

They began wrapping shrimp and fresh pineapple in bacon to put on skewers. Next, they seasoned the tenderloins and slid them into a hot oven. They tossed the asparagus on rimmed baking sheets and tore chunks of prosciutto over them before adding sliced almonds. Those went on the bottom oven racks. The kitchen felt muggy, even with the French doors open to let in a breeze off the lake, so Tessa turned on the air conditioning. She could feel her coppery hair grow frizzier every minute, even pulled back in a ponytail. They were mixing the crab spread when they heard the purr of a pontoon engine nearby.

Ian glanced out the windows, and his jaw clenched.

Tessa looked, too, to see what had aggravated him. One of Lily's friends stood at the steering wheel, and Lily stood next to him. She wore a cherry red bikini that was mostly strings with a few triangles of fabric attached. The man's hand was on her ass.

Ian yanked his cell phone out of his pocket. When Lily answered, he said, "What the hell are you doing? Are all of the tables set up with white tablecloths and are all of the dishes and glasses arranged?"

She gave a brief answer, and Ian's expression turned hostile. When he jammed the phone back in his pocket, he said, "Lily told Luther and Kayla what to do. Her friends wanted to see the lake."

Tessa didn't know what to say. This wasn't the time for Ian to lose his temper. He needed to pull off the open house. She settled on, "We're making great progress. If we keep going, at this rate, we'll have the food ready and you can get back to the lodge earlier than you expected."

He growled and reached for the small, fancy glasses to start assembling the shooters. She started work on the crostini. They plugged through all of the preparations, loaded the food into the trunk of Ian's car, and then separated to get ready for the party.

Tessa showered and dressed. When she looked at her reflection in the mirror, she did a double take. *Ugh*. Not good. She turned on music, grabbed a curling iron, and set out makeup. She'd be damned if she'd stand next to Lily looking like a pitiful lab specimen.

By the time she walked into Ian's resort, she had a bounce to her step, her hair was pulled up in a loose, casual knot, and she looked as good as she ever had. Ian, as always, had cleaned up to his usual, casual gorgeousness. He smiled when he saw her. "I like your dress."

"Thanks." The periwinkle-blue made her copper hair pop. She looked around the lobby. The sign-in desk had been turned into a bar with bottles of wine and beer. A table at the side of the room displayed the food. A table opposite held the desserts. Brochures listing all of the local farmers and specialty items spread across a side table. "It looks good. Classy."

Ian nodded, obviously happy with the results. "Yeah, no thanks to Lily, we pulled it off. It's exactly what I was hoping for."

Lily saw her and came to press herself against Ian's side. She wore a sparkly, rose-colored top and a short, white skirt. Very trendy. Her skin glowed. A boat ride will do that for you. "The food's wonderful, perfect for this occasion."

"Thanks."

Lily's friends drifted toward them. Lily made quick introductions before saying, "Tessa owns the bakery and produce stand down the road. She dropped out of college to run her grandparents' farm."

"I've heard about your pies and cakes," one of the men in the party said. He held up a beef tenderloin slider with southwest aioli. "This is delicious. Who needs accounting when you can cater and run a business?"

"The accounting helps keeps me practical." Tessa glanced around the room to search out Darinda or some other old friends. Small talk didn't rank high on her list of fun activities.

Lily gave a smug smile. "Tessa's a writer, too. She sells romances."

"Really?" a woman exclaimed. "How do you think of ideas?"

If Tessa had a nickel for every time someone asked that question . . . but the woman's interest was genuine. She tried to explain. "Once ideas start, they just keep coming. Once you open the flood gates, you get more than you need."

The woman stared. "Wait a minute. Ian said your last name is Lawrence. You're not T. A. Lawrence, are you? I've bought every one of your books."

Lily frowned. "Tessa's romances are mostly fantasy. She was engaged once, it didn't work, and she gave up on men."

Ian stared at her. "Tess is taking a sabbatical."

"For years and years!" Lily turned to her. "You have different locations for your series, though, don't you? I thought you never left Mill Pond."

Lily was clearly in a mood. What the hell was her problem? "My family loved to travel. We took trips every summer. These days, I'm invited to quite a few writers' conferences. Harmony—a fellow writer—and I meet up and explore together."

Lily slanted a glance to her friends. "So you're not the country bumpkin I thought you were."

"That's _enough_." Ian glared.

Lily looked up at him, surprised. "But we've hardly gotten to know Tessa better."

"Lucky her." Ian nodded across the room to Keavin. "Tess, he's been trying to catch your attention since you walked through the door. I'm sure you'll enjoy his company more than ours." He motioned Tessa away, and she gladly escaped. When she looked back at Lily later, she was with her group. Ian had left them to make the rounds, greeting his guests.

"The little cat showed her claws," Darinda whispered in Tessa's ear, coming to stand closer.

Keavin grinned. "Bet Ian hasn't seen that side of her before."

David came to wrap an arm around Tessa's shoulders. "You rattled her cage, girl, and she showed her true colors."

But the thought didn't make Tessa happy. Lily had drawn a line in the sand, and Ian would have to decide which side he would stand on. Tessa was one hundred percent sure, he'd choose Lily's.

As much as she enjoyed seeing her friends, she was relieved when four o'clock came and the open house started breaking up. It had been a big success. Everyone talked about the wonderful job Ian had done on the resort. Lily's friends took brochures with them to show to people they knew. The whole event had been an ordeal for Tessa. She drove home, glad it was over.

Even though it was still early, she slipped out of her clothes and into her pajamas. Her feet ached. She was ready to sip a glass of wine and rent a movie. She'd have to lay low for the next couple days. Lily was staying with Ian, and Tessa didn't want to run into her. She jabbed at the remote. She didn't relish the idea of cooking one lonely supper for herself tomorrow.

When she flipped on the TV, an ad for a huge three-day art festival in Columbus flashed visions of tents and food kiosks. Tessa liked art. She'd always meant to buy another painting for her living room, but the idea of wandering from one booth to the next, alone, didn't appeal to her. Darinda always complained that David would rather spend his free time in the den with his buddies, watching a game on TV—whatever the season offered—than attend an art show with her. Tessa picked up her phone and dialed Darinda's number. "I'm going to the art show in Columbus tomorrow. Want to come along?"

There was a pregnant pause. "Is this my friend, Tessa? The homebody who never leaves her property?"

Really. What was this? Pick on Tessa week? "Yup, it's me. I'm on my own tomorrow, and I'm in the mood to have fun. Is school still in session?"

"Friday was our last day. Does this have anything to do with Miss Blonde Bombshell nesting at Lakeview Stables?"

"Maybe."

"In that case, I'll be there. I'll pick you up at noon."

"I should drive," Tessa argued. "It was my idea."

"Girl, I love you, but there's no way I'm riding in that piece of junk pickup you're so fond of."

"You just don't know quality when you see it."

"Yes, I do. That's why I'm driving."

With her plans made, Tessa hung up with a smile.

She was still smiling when Darinda pulled to the door at noon on Monday.

"This is a great way for me to start my summer vacation!"

They gossiped on the hour-long drive to Columbus, ignoring the scenery they passed. Darinda couldn't find a place to park and had to pay to leave her SUV a distance away from the event. People crowded the streets. They walked five blocks before bursting onto the streets, ready to shop. Tents paraded up and down, offering jewelry, photography, fabrics, and paintings.

Tessa stopped at Randall Scott Hardin's tent to ogle an oil of a Broad Ripple night scene. Both she and Darinda knew that area of Indianapolis, and she was struck by the vivid touches of light and color. She winced at the price tag, but the painting was worth every penny, and soon, she and Darinda were loading it into the back of Darinda's SUV.

A shish kebab kiosk attracted them on the way back.

"We had a late breakfast, but I need something to eat," Darinda said. "All this shopping makes me hungry."

They nibbled as they walked down the street, peeking in tents. Darinda nodded toward three, young girls, teetering on stiletto heels and giggling together. "You can only wear shoes that high when you're young. At our age, you get nose bleeds."

They started people watching as much as shopping. Darinda pointed toward four twenty-something guys wearing jeans with holes in them, long hair, and tight T-shirts. "Bet they belong in a band."

Tessa smiled when girls turned to swoon over them. "I'm guessing you're right."

"Wonder what those girls would do if Ian and Brody walked past them. Faint?"

Tessa laughed. "Maybe Ian's in the wrong business. He should play drums."

They thought up silly scenarios as they visited other tents. Darinda found an outdoor sculpture for her patio, and they lugged it to the car. Then she turned to Tessa. "Enough with the art already. I need a new summer dress, something fun and sexy. And you need . . . a new wardrobe. Let's look at clothes."

Tessa blinked. "Am I that bad?"

"I've seen you in the same khakis for at least three years. Waste not, want not is great for some things, but hon, those pants have seen better days."

A vision of Lily sprang into Tessa's mind. She doubted that girl had one practical outfit in her wardrobe. "I want to turn heads."

"Damn, girl, this is gonna be fun!" Darinda led her to the small boutiques close to downtown.

Tessa quickly learned that khakis weren't going to cut it for week-end frippery. Darinda turned thumbs down for one outfit after another that she chose.

"You can buy basics for church socials," her friend told her. "But it's time to get a little groovy for when you go out."

Snug, colorful tops went onto the "to buy" piles, along with flirty skirts and shorts. Two hours later, both women returned to the SUV with bags overflowing.

"I need a drink." Darinda started toward the outdoor tables at a corner bar. "Just one beer to wet my whistle, and then we can head for home."

Tessa ordered fried pickles, along with her wine. As they munched, they avoided any topics that hinted at weighty. By the time they turned back for Mill Pond, Darinda sighed. "I can't remember the last time I had so much fun with a girlfriend. We need to do this again."

"Works for me."

"I'm holding you to that. Between my kids and your barn and books, we hardly spend any time together. It's time we do girls' days out more often." Darinda stopped at a red light. She glanced at Tessa, then glanced away. "I know you're not going to like this, and I'll only say it once, then let it drop, but David and I have been talking about you and Ian. And we both think you'd be better for him than Lily. I say, kick that girl to the curb and grab that man for yourself."

Tessa sighed. "You know I can't do that. Ian's trying to talk Lily into moving in with him. But that's why I came here today. It's time I start thinking about what I want next."

"You'd be doing Ian a favor if you saved him from Bubbly Blonde." At Tessa's grimace, Darinda said, "Okay, subject dropped. Let Ian drown in his own misery. But what about you? What are you going to do now?"

The words "doing Ian a favor" stuck in Tessa's mind. That's what Grams said about Sadie, that Sadie had done her a favor by snagging Gary. *Bull pucky.* If Sadie hadn't shown up, she and Gary would still be happy together. She took a deep breath. "We both knew Ian was just a kick in the pants to get me out of my own, little world. It worked. Now I have to move on. Hell, even Grams has found someone new."

Darinda laughed. "Yeah, I heard. I'm happy for her and Miguel. For you, though, it's time to pull on your big girl panties and find yourself a man."

Even big girl panties couldn't work miracles. "Easy enough to say, but I know every man in the entire area. The good ones are taken, and the others . . . well, I've known them too long."

"We'll think of something." Darinda reached for the CD player. They sang along to songs she'd recorded on their drive home. And by the time she dropped Tessa back at her front porch, and they'd unloaded all her goodies, Tessa had built up her courage to meet the next challenge in her life, head-on.

Chapter 22

Tessa kept herself busy on Tuesday. She worked in the barn in the morning, canning rhubarb jam and freezing rhubarb pies. She had more rhubarb than ever before. She even froze stalks of it to use later. In the evening, she did something she'd never done before. She went online to look at dating sites.

There were more people listed than she'd ever imagined. She'd heard the horror stories, but there were more stories of success. How many miles would she drive to meet someone? And what kind of man did she want to meet? No one, really. She wanted Ian. But he was taken, so she scanned other men's faces and bios. Some sounded good. Some sounded *too* good, but they didn't have black hair and chocolate-brown eyes. Their smiles didn't have a naughty sauciness about them. She turned off the computer with a sigh.

On Wednesday morning, Kayla came for her baking lesson. Tessa decided to start with simple recipes and work their way into more difficult ones. They made square pans of gingerbread and Polish apple cakes. For small, dainty desserts, Tessa taught Kayla how to make tiny cream puffs. They filled a dozen with homemade pastry cream and sprinkled them with powdered sugar. Kayla carried a sampling of each home with her when she left.

"Luther's going to love these." She held the carriers gently. "What are you going to do with the extras?"

Tessa grinned. "I'm keeping them in the cooler for Grams. She's taking them to church to serve with coffee on Sunday."

"That's right. You two bake tomorrow, don't you? Do you need me?"

Tessa shook her head. "No, Grams and I can handle the bakery business. I was thinking you and I could bake for Ian, Monday through

Wednesday, and Grams and I can bake on Thursday." She hesitated. "Would it bother you if I hired a high school kid to sell stuff at the farm stand?"

Kayla looked relieved. "No, that way I can spend more time in the gardens."

"Good, it's settled then. You can bake and do yard work. That will keep you busy enough."

Kayla left with a happy bounce in her step. Tessa smiled, watching her. Then she called Grams and told her that she needed a teenager to work the stand. Grams knew anyone and everyone. She'd pick the right person. When Ian came for supper, he looked happy, too.

"Damn, it feels good being here. I can relax when I'm with you." Lily had left in the morning, and she must have kept him busy. He sagged onto a stool at the kitchen island and watched her stir shrimp in a large skillet. "What did you make for me tonight?"

He sounded cocky. "You've been spoiled enough, haven't you? You probably ate out every night with Lily."

He grinned. "That's restaurant food. It's different. I've missed coming here. Your kitchen is always full of good smells. It's comfortable. I can unwind."

Her heart did a happy little skip, but she ignored it. She was not Sadie. Ian was off limits. She'd found a few promising men on the dating sites. She'd message them. They'd take her mind off Ian. "I went simple for supper—shrimp scampi over spaghetti and a tossed salad."

"Perfect." He leaned forward, resting his elbows on the counter top. "What have you been up to the last few days?" His gaze traveled up and down her body, lingered on her face.

Her insides melted, or at least, that's what it felt like. Ian's gaze could make her pulse do rumbas. Jeez, she'd missed him. She busied herself, tossing the salad, while she told him about Kayla learning to help her in the bakery. She rambled on about Grams getting more tired when they worked together and how Grams was going to have Sunday suppers at her little house in town from now on.

Ian listened to her, hanging on every word she said. His expression clouded. "You're going to miss Grams on Sundays. You two get along so well together."

"Yeah, but things change. She isn't getting any younger, and she and Miguel are a perfect pair."

Ian studied her face. "Your grandpa was perfect for her, too, wasn't he? It's hard to find that kind of connection."

"True. Grams is lucky. She found it twice."

His voice bleak, Ian asked, "Do you believe a person only has one soul mate, and if they miss their chance to connect with that person, they have to settle for less?"

Tessa blinked. Where had that come from? "I sure hope not. There are a lot of people in the world. It would be hard to find the one and only that was meant for you."

Ian circled the island to help her dish-up their food. When his arm brushed hers, he turned and looked down at her. Her breath caught in her throat, and she couldn't back away from him. They were too close together.

She gazed into his chocolate-brown eyes, held by the emotion in their depths. He bent his head, and his lips grazed hers. Heat sizzled through her veins, made her nerves sing for more.

He pulled back quickly, and when he spoke, his voice was thick with need. "I can't come here anymore."

Every fiber in her body wanted to attach itself to his. She had to lock her hands behind her back to keep from reaching for him. She wanted to stand on tiptoe, to crush his mouth with her own. Shame shouted in her mind. She *was* Sadie, no better. If Ian took her in his arms right now, she'd toss thoughts of Lily aside. She'd meet his passion with her own. She took a shaky breath. Oh, how she wanted him. But he'd just said the responsible thing. He couldn't come here anymore.

Trying to keep her voice steady, she asked, "Are you going to open the lodge for business? You won't have time for much of anything then."

He stepped away from her, shook his head. "Lily decided to move in with me. When I worked in the city, I didn't mind just seeing her on weekends. But here . . ." He looked at Tessa and looked away. "Well, I need to spend more time with her."

Hurt clotted inside her, settled in a pool of misery in her soul, but she refused to acknowledge it. She'd miss him, but if they kept spending evenings together, they'd both be disappointed in themselves. She forced a smile. "I'm happy for you."

His brows knit together. "Are you? What are you going to do with your extra time?"

She pointed to the laptop on her kitchen table. "I've watched you and Lily, how happy you are together." They were, right? "And I've decided I'm missing out. I'm going modern."

He looked like she'd slapped him. He took a deep breath. "You're going to move in with someone, too?"

She shook her head. "I'm joining some dating sites to try to connect."

He didn't say anything, just stared out the kitchen window for a minute. Finally, he squared his shoulders and said, "That's good. You'll have to beat guys away. A friend of mine in the city met his wife on a dating service."

His voice sounded strained. She decided to change the subject. "So, how did the test run go for the lodge?"

"What?"

"The lodge, the guests that spent the weekend . . . how did that go?"

He ran a hand through his dark hair. "Great, everything went great."

He helped her carry their plates to the sunroom to eat. He sat on one side of the room. She sat a good distance away. They picked at their food until he said, "Well, I'd better go. Lily wants our room redecorated before she moves in Friday night." He stood and jammed his hands deep in his jeans pockets. "Tess . . ."

She shook her head. "You're one of the best friends I've ever had. I don't want anything to ruin that."

He pressed his lips into a tight line and gave a curt nod. "I'd better go." He didn't even stay to help with cleanup. He hurried out the door.

She cleaned the kitchen on autopilot, then did what she rarely allowed herself. She walked to the lake, sat on the shore, and cried until she ran out of tears.

Chapter 23

S he looked like hell on Thursday morning. Grams took one look at her face and shook her head. "I heard. The snot's moving in with him."

"That's good. I need a reason to keep my distance."

"Why's that?"

"I don't want to be a Sadie. Ian's too easy to like. And he likes me back."

"That's a problem?" Grams started measuring ingredients for pie dough. "Look, hon, you and Gary were great friends, but there was no spark between you. It would be like you shacking up with Keavin. You like him. You care about him. So why didn't you two run off together?"

"It's not like that between us, never was. We're just friends."

"So were you and Gary—friends. Sadie did you a big favor. She saved you from taking the safe route, and she put a lot of pizzazz in Gary's life."

Tessa stared. "I loved Gary."

"You love your brother, too. Big deal. I, personally, would want a lot more."

Tessa dumped a half cup of salt in her cake batter instead of sugar. She stared. A stupid mistake. She went to the sink and dumped the batter. She'd have to start again. "Okay, maybe I need to rethink things, but Ian loves Lily. She has plenty of pizzazz."

"But they don't have anything in common." Grandma reached out to stop Tessa's hand before she added salt to her batter again. "Look, kid, a good marriage needs people who share common beliefs *and* share some sizzle. It takes both. You and Gary cared about the same things, but there was no spark, no chemistry. Ian and Lily have lots of chemistry, but nothing in common. Fifty percent isn't enough."

"They both work hard, play hard," Tessa said.

Grams sighed. "Look. You don't want to be a homewrecker. I get that, but Lily won't make Ian happy. And vice versa."

Tessa felt her expression turn mutinous. Her grandmother knew that look. She'd complained about it often. "Ian has to figure that out for himself."

"Then he's in trouble, because he's like Gary. He wouldn't cheat unless someone helped him along."

"Sadie."

"Like I said, Sadie did you a big favor, kid. It didn't feel like it at the time, but she did."

Tessa went to the cupboard to get cocoa powder. She didn't want to talk about it anymore. Answers that seemed solid now looked like questions. Her mind was a morass of confusion. Grams understood. When Tessa came back, they switched on music and baked like maniacs for the rest of the day.

Before Grams left, she gave Tessa a warm hug. "Hang in there, girl. Life's throwing you a few curves lately. I'd tell you to enjoy the ride, but it's been damn bumpy." She stopped. "I did help you with one problem, though. I have a new kid hired to help at the stand. Kayla can train him tomorrow."

Tessa grimaced. "Let me guess. He's moody and his teachers would like to send him to boarding school."

Grams smiled. "What better recommendations could a kid have?"

She should have known. Grams only took in strays. But if Grams liked the kid, there was something worth working with somewhere. "Okay, I'll see you both tomorrow."

Tessa stalked to the house and glowered at the familiar setting. She wasn't in the mood to eat alone and stew about Ian. She wasn't in the mood to drive to the diner and answer questions from friends, either. She paced back and forth. Where could she go and just relax? Chase's bar—Mill Pond's sort of nightclub.

She changed into her good jeans and one of her new, flirty tops. She let her thick hair out of its scrunchy, so that it hung loose, and drove to the bar for supper. People called and nodded to her when she walked inside. Evan Meyers and his wife waved her over to eat supper with them. When they'd finished their food, the music started, and Keavin came to ask her to dance. Tessa loved to dance. Once her feet started moving, she turned into an uninhibited, feel-the-beat, wild woman. Men came to drag her onto the dance floor until she fizzled at ten.

"Sorry," she told Chase Carlton, her last partner. "I have to open the bakery tomorrow morning. I've got to get home and get some sleep. And shouldn't you get back behind the bar?"

"But the next song's a slow one. You can't leave me stranded for that." Chase pulled her closer. The band took his cue and shifted tempo.

Oh, what the hell? She was having fun. Tessa let him smash her closer as they swayed to the music. Then his hand cupped her ass. Big deal. If that was his thrill for the night, poor him. He knew he wasn't going to get lucky with her, and that's what he was known for. Chase tended bar here and was known as a player. If a woman wanted a good lay, she ordered drinks and flirted with Chase. He'd deserted his post to share two dances with her.

"You're single. I'm single. Why haven't we ever connected?" he whispered in her ear.

"I'd worry about catching a disease."

He threw back his head and laughed. "I get regular penicillin shots. I stay clean."

"How romantic. Now you have me interested."

He grinned. "I've always liked you, Tessa Lawrence. Maybe we should just have a fling."

"Isn't that what you always do?"

He pulled slightly apart to study her. "I'm getting older. So are you. Maybe we should think about shacking up."

No wonder the women loved him. Such a way with words. "Yeah, you'd love weeding gardens and pickling vegetables."

"They say opposites attract."

She smiled. "That, they do. But they don't last. It's like a chemistry experiment that blows up in your face."

"Do you have an answer for everything?"

"Annoying isn't it? See? We're not meant for each other."

He laughed. "Well, I'm going to enjoy it while I can." He smashed her to him and put both hands on her ass.

Enjoyment worked two ways. It had been a long time since a guy felt her up. Tessa leaned into him and went with it.

Chapter 24

Grams raced into the barn on Friday morning, a big grin on her face. "The news is all over town."

Tessa shrugged. "Mill Pond needs to find more to talk about."

"Did you really dance, cheek to cheek, with Chase Carlton?"

"No cheeks were involved. My boobs were smashed against his chest, and his hands groped my ass, but we never made cheek contact."

Grams laughed. "It's about time! No one knows what to think. Chase told everyone he'd asked you to marry him."

"I'm not sure shacking up is the same as marriage."

Tessa could tell Grams loved it. "What a way to let the world know you're ready to spread your wings. I couldn't have done it better myself. Rumor is all the single guys in Mill Pond are ready to start courting."

Tessa groaned. "That's not what I had in mind."

"Oh, hell, enjoy it. Tarnish your reputation a little more if you can. It's been spotless too long."

Tessa shook her head and walked to the door to turn the sign to OPEN. People rushed into the shop. One of them was Ian, who glared at her, grabbed her arm, and pulled her to one side. Not one person went to the glass cases. They all milled around, looking innocent, clearly trying their best to eavesdrop on their conversation.

"Is it true you're going to marry Chase Carlton?"

"What?" Tessa stared at him. "Where did you hear that?"

"I drove to Garth's Gas Station to buy gas for the riding mower this morning. Garth said the rumor's flying all over town."

Tessa sighed. "He only gave me a friendship ring. We thought we'd fool around first to see if we're sexually compatible." Mouths dropped open and when Ian growled, Tessa laughed. "Don't believe everything you hear. I danced with Chase last night. That's all."

"That's not what I heard. I heard he was wearing you like a second skin."

Okay, now he'd gone too far. Tessa could feel her temper rising. "This is my place of business. You realize that, don't you? Not the best spot to have this discussion."

He glanced at the other people in the shop and had the grace to look contrite.

She pressed her point. "I wouldn't think of storming into your lodge and making a scene in front of your guests."

Ian ran a hand through his dark hair. "I'm sorry. I didn't think. I heard the rumors, heard the gossip about Chase, and came unglued."

Grams nodded at him. "That Chase is a charmer, for sure. A good dancer, too. Lots of moves."

Tessa threw her a dirty look. She wasn't helping. Not that it made much difference. Most of the people milling around had already heard the gossip and hurried in for more. It would be good for business if nothing else.

Ian's jaw tightened. "Are you interested in this guy?"

"What's it to you? You roll under the sheets with your fiancée. I don't lecture you about premarital sex."

People moved closer.

"We've been engaged for eight months."

"So what? When did you start doing it?"

Ian glanced helplessly at his fellow customers, and they all busied themselves, studying the prices of jams and jellies. "I just don't want you to rush into anything and make a mistake. You know, the rebound effect."

"Because I can't have you? I knew that from the beginning." She started toward the cash register, but he reached for her again. She would have put him in his place, but he looked so upset, it surprised her.

"You know, and I know, that things got a little out of hand. I care about you more than I should. That's why Lily decided to move in early. Either that, or . . ." He closed his eyes, frustrated.

She put a hand on his arm. "You're a good man. You'd never cheat on Lily. I like that about you."

He visibly fought for calm. "That doesn't mean you have to turn into a manizer."

"What?" She blinked.

"Men are womanizers, right? You don't have to go through a string of guys to get over me."

She let out a huff of air. "Is that what you think? You're a little full of yourself! Maybe I'm tired of being the good girl. Maybe I'm tired of not getting any. I might want to spread my wings and see what's out there."

"No!"

People leaned forward to hear better.

Tessa looked at them. If they wanted a show, well, they'd get one. "It's true, guys. A man broke my heart and I came here to heal. I'm whole now. Ian helped me realize that. I want a shot at true love, but I'm not interested in anyone around here. I've known you all too long. I'm trying a dating service."

Heads nodded in approval.

Ian looked at Grams. "Tell her. Tell her she's only going to get hurt again."

Grams shrugged. "What's she gotten by playing it safe?"

"I want to meet the guy you settle on." He made it sound like it was his God-given right. "I'll set him straight. If he hurts you, I'll . . ."

Tessa reached up and rubbed a hand on his cheek. *Mmm, stubble.* She loved stubble. "Did your sisters let you pick their husbands?"

He blinked. "No."

"Did you take Lily to get their approval?"

"No."

"It doesn't work that way, but thank you for caring. You're not my big brother. You're a friend. Know your boundaries."

Hands balled into fists, he stomped to the door. "You deserve the best. Don't settle for less."

"Thank you."

When the door slammed behind him, Tessa walked behind the counter to ring up orders.

Iris Clinger, the town's real estate agent, pointed randomly at a cake and said, "I'll take that one." She wiped a tear from her cheek. "I've never seen anything so romantic in my whole life. That boy loves you."

"We're best friends, like brother and sister."

"If you say so, hon. The first time I saw him, I knew he was right for Lakeview Stables. And seeing you two together, I know he's right for you." Iris took her cake, and plenty of people filed up behind her in line.

Tessa sighed. It was going to be a long day. By the time the last person left the shop, over two-thirds of her customers had voted for her and Ian eloping together. She should have listened to her own advice. If you farted sideways in Mill Pond, everyone knew.

People came and went all day, and they'd all heard the gossip. By the time she and Grams locked the barn and headed for home, that's all anyone had talked about. Tessa should have been annoyed. She wasn't. She'd never thought she was capable of being scandalous. It was good to know she might have it in her.

When Grams walked to her car, she called, "This is the first day of June. You might want to check your horoscope for the month. You've started it with a bang."

Tessa thought about that. Maybe it was time something shook up her life. She could drive to the diner tonight for supper and really get gossip flying. But her feet hurt. And she'd listened to gossip all day. On second thought, she turned toward her nice, comfortable bungalow and decided to stir things up when she had more energy.

When she sat on the front porch in the evening, enjoying a small breeze, she reconsidered her decision. A moving van drove down the county road. Lily's things—she was moving in with Ian tonight. The pain started in her chest and spread. But if Grams was right, Sadie had done her a favor. And so had Ian. He'd made her realize everything she was missing. It was going to hurt for a while, losing him. She'd give herself a week or two to lick her wounds. But then she'd be stronger and smarter. Somewhere, out there, was someone who was right for her. Someone who had similar beliefs and plenty of sizzle. She meant to find him.

Chapter 25

On Monday afternoon, Ian called Tessa. "I know Kayla comes to bake with you on Monday mornings. Luther told me, so I waited to call. But do you know anything about horses?"

"Not really, we never owned any."

He hesitated. "Well, I'm buying some for my stables, and I have an expert with me, but I thought you might have some advice."

"Get a few who don't spook and are good around people. Most of your guests will want to ride horses, but they won't know how to."

"Right. I'll keep that in mind." He stalled. "Sorry about the scene I made at your bakery. I had no business—"

She cut him off. "The customers loved it, but never do it again."

"Right." He seemed at a loss for words. "You should know, I'm opening the lodge next Monday, so I'll need your baked goods for the dining room."

"Gotcha. I'll be ready. Have you decided what you want—cakes, pies, puddings?"

"I was going to let you pick. I liked the idea of afternoon teas. Whatever works with that. We're booked, though. There's four rooms on the second floor and four more on the third. And the cabins are full. About thirty or forty people? I'll check on how many kids are coming with parents."

"Are you settled in?"

"Yeah, Lily and I made the right wing off the main house into our private quarters, and my chef—Paula—and her two kids have the left wing. She's moving in tomorrow. Once she's here, you can check menus with her, if you want."

"Sounds perfect." Her heart clenched—Lily would be waking up next to Ian in the mornings, sipping coffee with him before they got dressed for the day. But no, not true. Lily traveled most of the time. She'd only spoon into him on weekend nights. But he was hers. The ache settled deeper.

He hesitated. "How's everything with you?"

"Busy, but falling into place. I like working with Kayla."

Another pause. "Well, I know we're both going to be swamped soon, but I don't want to be strangers. Take care, Tess."

"I will. You, too."

It felt odd to hang up on such a nothing conversation with him. It was for the best, though. Lily would be with Ian on weekends, and he'd be busy with the lodge during the week. And she'd stay busy, too. She'd make sure of that.

The evening stretched before her, though, alone in a house that suddenly felt too empty. She called Keavin and invited him over for supper. Then she went to the barn and made so much cookie dough ahead, she might not use it all for a month.

When Keavin came at six, the aroma of Hungarian goulash greeted him. He knocked on the screen door, then let himself in. "I'm following my nose to the kitchen!" He grinned as he handed Tessa a bottle of wine and she handed him a bottle of cold beer. "You remembered."

She laughed. "I hope your taste hasn't changed. This used to be your favorite."

"Still is." He plopped on a stool at the kitchen counter. "So, I heard your boyfriend's fiancée moved in with him."

"He's not my boyfriend."

"He should be. I met Lily."

Tessa frowned at him. "Tearing her down isn't going to make me feel better."

Keavin took a long slurp of beer. "Oh, I like her. She's fun, but when the going gets tough, he's going to be on his own."

"We don't really know her." Tessa poured herself a glass of wine and sat across from him. "How's your dad and mom?"

"Dad's dying. Mom's in denial. It's uncomfortable, but everyone handles things differently. I'm glad Chelsea and I are moving back here. Mom's going to need us."

"If you need anything . . ."

"Same goes for you." He tipped his beer in her direction. "You going to be okay?"

"I'm going to miss Ian. He used to drop by almost every day, but I've lived alone for a while now. I'll get back in the swing."

Keavin gave a rueful smile. "You know, every summer when you came to visit your grandma and grandpa, I waited for you to notice me. Really notice me. I had such a big crush on you, but you never saw me that way."

Tessa felt herself color with embarrassment, and she bit her bottom lip. "I'm sorry."

He shook his head. "I lived through my teenage angst, went to college, made a life for myself, and met Chelsea. When she noticed me, I felt the earth move beneath my feet." He laughed. "Corny, I know, but that's what it felt like. Ian did that for you."

"I know, but I'll move on, too, just like you did."

"Don't hide away this time, Tessie."

"I'm not planning to."

He nodded. "Good, then my best-friend lecture is done. We can enjoy ourselves."

And they did. But when Keavin left, Tessa wondered. Why hadn't she looked at Keavin and seen him in a different light? He was smart, funny, and caring. Why Ian? Why was he the one who got to her when she could ignore most men?

She poured herself another glass of wine and walked to the TV set. The more she thought about romance, the less she understood it. Her best bet, she decided, was to *not* think about it. She'd lick her wounds, get through this, and find someone else.

Tuesday, however, proved to be a long day. She and Kayla baked in the morning, then Tessa ran to town to prowl the aisles of the grocery store. Her cupboards were growing bare. She stopped in at Grams' house on the way home, and then finally had to return to a quiet, empty house.

Maybe she should get a pet? She'd had a cat when she was growing up. Cats were less work than dogs. She went to her computer and was looking through pictures of sad-looking cats at the shelter when a car pulled into her drive.

Darinda, David, and the boys spilled into her house, bearing a large pan of lasagna.

"Girl, this is going to be your worst week," Darinda said. "So we came to keep your mind off running into the hills to become a hermit."

It was impossible to pout with two friends and two boys clamoring for attention. By the time they left, Tessa was dead on her feet. But she almost teared up when she glanced at herself in the mirror while she brushed her teeth for bed. How lucky was she to have friends like that?

On Wednesday, Kayla baked alongside her, chattering more than usual as they worked. Even she was outdoing herself to keep Tessa's mind off Ian. After they put away the last bowl and cookie sheet, she didn't leave, but stalled around long enough that she was still there when Ian's new chef came to talk business.

When Tessa saw her, she tried not to show her surprise. Kayla glanced at her and blinked, obviously a little dumbfounded, too.

Paula gave a wry smile. "I know, I don't quite fit in, but Ian swears people will get used to me." The woman was about five-two with long hair dyed pitch black and clipped up in a modern twist to make a jagged fringe across the back of her head. Black eyeliner rimmed sapphire-blue eyes, and she wore a nose ring. Tattoos covered her arms, her neck, and her ankles.

Tessa laughed. "We don't see a lot of Goths around here, but there's always a first." She held out a hand. "It's nice to meet you. This is my helper, Kayla."

Paula turned her attention to the girl. "I heard that you made my life a little easier. You came up with the afternoon tea idea, right? That way, I only have to worry about a soup, salad, and tea sandwiches every day for lunch."

Kayla's blush spread from her throat all the way to her root line. "Tessa taught me how to bake fancy little treats. I didn't realize how much work they were."

Paula chuckled. "You've got that right. Bite-size stuff's a bother. Now, what about your gardens? Can I get fresh produce here every day?"

"If we have it." Relief niggled through Tessa. She appreciated all her friends' efforts to keep her emotionally afloat, but it was nice not to have to deal with Ian's aftermath for a minute.

Paula pulled a notebook out of her bag. "I brought menu ideas for my first month here. Do you have time to look at them with me?"

Kayla inched toward the door. "Since you're busy . . ."

"I'll see you later. Thanks for everything." Tessa watched her leave before settling over the menus with Paula. Once she got over the distraction of a small stud that twinkled in Paula's lip, she got down to work. When they finished, Tessa smiled. "You shouldn't have any problems getting supplies. You should be in good shape. Are you settled in at the lodge? How do you like the place?"

"The lodge is great. I love the work, and Ian's a considerate boss, just a little on the moody side."

"Ian?" Tessa stared. "He's one of the most easy-going people I've met."

"If you say so. Maybe he's just uptight about getting everything right for the grand opening, but I never know if he's going to be in a good mood or brooding." Paula shrugged. "My husband was moody, too. I learned how to work around him, so it's no big deal."

Tessa grimaced. She remembered that Paula had two children, no husband, but the details were fuzzy. She couldn't concentrate as well as usual. "You're a widow?"

"My husband was a lifer in the military. Did two overseas tours. Didn't make it back from his last one."

"I'm sorry."

"When you marry a military guy, you always know it might happen. He didn't like sitting behind a desk. This job couldn't have come at a better time. The kids and I needed a fresh start. The job includes room and board, so I might even be able to save up a little."

Fresh starts. There seemed to be lot of that going around lately. Tessa nodded. "We're going to get along just fine, I can tell. It'll be nice working with you."

By the time Paula left, Tessa knew what she'd need to provide each day for a month, both for produce, teas, and desserts. Paula promised to send someone over to collect them every evening.

A good thing. Then Tessa wouldn't have to go to the lodge. She could take a breath, gather her courage, and heal.

Chapter 26

Tessa hardly saw Ian for the next few weeks, and when she did, it wasn't the same. He was withdrawn, different. As she suspected, he spent most of his waking hours dealing with guests and business . . . and most of his weekends, dealing with Lily.

After the first miserable week, each day got a little better. After all, she'd seen what was coming. Part of her was prepared for it. Sort of. She still kept busy during the days, but started looking online at dating services in the evenings.

Somewhere, near the end of June, she drove to Columbus to have supper with a new man she'd met online. "We're both on the rebound," he'd written her. "Bodes badly for us working out, but we might enjoy dinner together."

She'd dressed in one of the outfits Darinda had helped her pick out—a white, peasant blouse and a short, bouncy skirt. She'd taken time with her hair and make-up. All in all, she looked better than usual. She walked to the outdoor café where they'd agreed to meet, saw the red, button-down shirt and purple, baseball cap he'd said he'd wear, and headed to meet him. The shirt was expensive, she noticed. So was everything about him. He rose to greet her, and when she looked up from the seat he offered her, there were Ian and Lily seated on the other side of the café's big, glass window.

Tessa forced a smile and a small wave, then turned her attention back to her date. He glanced to where she'd looked and grinned. "Your friend has some looker on his arm, doesn't he? Bet she's a firecracker."

Tessa bit the inside of her cheek. Not a good start. She didn't like this guy already. She tried for small talk. "I've never been to this café. What's it known for?"

He took a sip of his martini. "It's one of those trendy places that offers crab cakes and filet mignon sliders, fancy wines, and special ales, but mostly, it's a place to see and be seen. I want the bitch I was dating to know I've met someone else."

Tessa leaned back in her chair, her shoulders stiff. "That's why you posted on the dating site? You said you were on the rebound, not stuck in revenge mode. How did I get so lucky? Why did you choose my profile?"

"Who could miss you with all that copper hair?" He gave a tight smile when a car slowed as it passed them, the wife turning in the passenger seat to gawk at them. "See? That's one of Desiree's best friends. She'll spread the news the minute she can pull out her cell phone."

"At least you're honest." Tessa picked up the menu. She usually ordered moderately priced meals on a first date, but this guy might as well pay for whatever struck her fancy. "I think I'll have a crab cake for an appetizer and lobster for my entrée."

He grinned. "I like that. You've decided to make me pay for my sins. I'm not intrigued by women who are easy. By the way, I'm Aaron. I think it's going to be a pleasure to meet you."

"Don't count on it. This will be our one and only date."

His blue eyes sparkled. "You're more interesting than I expected. Your little ditty on the matchmaking site made you sound too goody-goody to be true. You own a farm stand and a bakery. Really."

"I *do* run a farm stand and a bakery."

"But you're no little Miss Sweetness, are you? There's fire under that sugar coating."

She sighed. "I'm not going to duel with you to earn my supper. If I have to, I can pay for my own. I'm here. I'm hungry, and we can either have a nice evening, or you can take a hike."

He laughed. "Warning noted. I'll be on my best behavior."

And he was, but he'd already ruined it for Tessa. They talked about books, movies, and places they'd traveled, but she didn't trust him. When they were waiting for their coffee and dessert to arrive, Ian and Lily left the restaurant and stopped at their table.

"Isn't this a wonderful restaurant?" Lily's smile upped to megawatts. Her gaze settled on Tessa's date, and her expression showed approval . . . and interest.

Ian's jaw tightened. He glared at Tessa. "If we'd known you were driving to Columbus, we could have offered you a ride."

Tessa couldn't hide her horror. An hour in the back seat, watching Ian and Lily exchange glances and touches. How special. She licked dry lips. "I had no idea you were coming."

"Have you two known each other long?" Lily's gaze connected with Aaron's.

Aaron grinned. "It's our first official meeting. I saw Tessa on a dating site and knew I'd spotted someone interesting." He leveled a look at Ian. "She's even more intriguing than I'd expected."

Ian's lips pressed together in a scowl.

Aaron looked even more amused. "And you two?" he asked Lily. "Are you old friends?"

Tessa shook her head. "They're engaged. Let me introduce you to Ian McGregor and his fiancée, Lily." She didn't know Lily's last name.

Aaron's voice turned silky as he smiled at Lily. "It's a pleasure to meet you."

Tessa turned a cold gaze his way. The man was enjoying himself too much at their expense.

Ian bristled. He put an arm through Lily's and said, "Well, it was nice seeing you, Tess. We'll leave you to your date." And he stalked off, taking Lily with him.

Aaron studied Tessa. "My, my, you *are* an interesting woman. I thought your boyfriend was going to take a swing at me."

"He's not my boyfriend. He's my neighbor. And he's engaged."

"Does his fiancée know that? I should have asked for her number. I might have gotten it."

Tessa bit back a reply. Tonight had been a total bust. The waiter came with their key lime pie and coffees, and she tried to force herself to eat. When they'd finished their meal and Aaron had paid, he laughed at her attempt to be polite.

"You didn't plan this," he told her, "so it's not your fault. I, on the other hand, was a total prick and tried to use you to make my ex jealous. But I haven't had so much fun for a long time. Thank you for helping me get over Desiree. She's not worth the bother. Neither is your friend's fiancée. She'll cheat on him. Hope he gets smart."

Tessa blinked. "She just moved in with him."

"And she's already flirting? Poor sod."

Why Tessa felt the need to stick up for Lily, she didn't know, but she didn't like the idea of Ian getting hurt. "Some people just flirt. Lily's like that."

Aaron shook his head. "If you gave me her number—which you won't, because you're too nice—and I called her, she'd hook up with me. I know women. She's a sure thing."

The thought troubled her. Lily didn't strike her as the "till death do us part" type, but Tess didn't think she'd cheat on Ian unless it was mutual. Still Aaron's comments worried her. But did he know women as well as he thought he did? Didn't he just get dumped by his ex?

Aaron pushed away from the table and reached for Tessa's hand. "I'll walk you to your car. If times were different, I'd ask you out again, but neither of us are in the best place for that, are we?"

When they reached her beat-up pickup, he stared. "I should have known. Not what I expected."

She slid behind the steering wheel and smiled a goodbye. "Thanks for the supper, Aaron. And good luck. I hope you meet the right person."

His grin surprised her. "But I'm always tempted by the not-so-nice ones, aren't I? Maybe in five years, if you're still single, I'll give you a call. By then, I should be ready."

She thought about that on her drive home. In five years, if she was still single, she might take him up on his offer. But she didn't want to wait that long.

On Thursday, when Grams was ready to leave after a day of baking, she shook a finger at Tessa. "I know Aaron didn't go that well, but don't give up. Keep trying. I've never seen you this moody, not even after you caught Gary cheating."

"I'm not moody."

"The hell, you're not. It's about time. You've been plastering fake smiles on your face for too long. Go out and get happy."

So Tessa tried. She drove into Columbus every once in a while to meet men who sounded interesting online for lunch or drinks. That's why it surprised her when Ian showed up at her house one night. She'd planned on running into town to grab supper from the diner, but her pickup wouldn't start. She turned the key, pumped the gas, and Gerty sputtered and groaned, but wouldn't turn over. She lifted the hood, got her hands dirty, but no luck. She added water to the radiator and was checking for a loose wire when she heard Ian's golf cart pull into her drive.

"Problems?" he asked.

"I'm going to have to get her towed. Maybe the battery or starter died. Garth can check the old girl over."

"Does she have a name?"

"Gerty." Tessa patted her fender.

"You've never thought of getting a second car as backup, just in case?"

Tessa blinked at him. How could he suggest such a thing? "That would be like admitting I couldn't trust her. That would just be wrong."

He laughed. "I could hear her suffering all the way from my place. I think she needs some TLC. Do you need a ride someplace?"

"It can wait. I'll give Garth a call, and he'll have someone pick her up."

Ian looked at his watch. "It's six o'clock. Have you eaten yet?"

He knew she hadn't. Six o'clock was when they used to get together for meals. "I was going to grab something from the diner."

"When I moved to Mill Pond, this nice neighbor rescued me when I was stranded on the side of the road, and she offered me supper. I'd like to return the favor."

Tessa grimaced. They'd done such a good job of avoiding each other—they hadn't seen one another for weeks. "Thanks anyway, but I can rummage for something in the refrigerator."

"No need to. I'll get my car and we can grab something together."

She bit her bottom lip, unsure. "What about the resort?"

"Paula and the waiters are serving supper. People are settled. No one will miss me for an hour or two."

She took a deep breath. This wasn't a good idea. She was just getting over him.

Ian grinned. "I'm not going to make any moves on you. We've both moved on. I'd still like to be your friend. Think of me as Keavin."

Oh, what the hell? They were neighbors. Mill Pond was too small a community to think they'd never bump into each other. She might as well learn how to cope. She hopped on the golf cart and rode back to the lodge with him. He called to Luther that he'd be gone for a while, led her to his car, and they drove into town. He stopped at Garth's first, and Garth promised he'd send someone for Gerty.

Folks stared when they walked into the diner together. Ian shrugged his shoulders and addressed the diners. "Her pickup died. She needed a ride. We're neighbors."

People nodded and returned their attention to their meals.

Ian shook his head. "Nothing goes unnoticed here, does it?"

"Not a thing." Tessa smiled. "How's life been for you? Business is good?"

"We've had a better start-up than I expected. The open house helped. Lily's friends told their friends, and we've had lots of reservations."

That, she knew from the amount of baked goods he bought from her each day, but it seemed like a safe topic to start with. "Do you enjoy it as much as you thought you would?"

"Even more."

The waitress came and they placed their orders. The weather was warm now, and heavy meals didn't appeal to her. Tessa ordered a BLT with a side salad.

Ian nodded. "That sounds good. I'll have the same thing." When she closed the menu, he stared at her hands. "Your fingernails are worse than usual. What would your mother say?"

"What Mom doesn't know won't hurt her."

"But she suspects."

She shot him a look. "You garden every day and see how manicured you look."

"Did you notice that Luther did more landscaping around the building? The boy knows his stuff. You taught him well."

She'd noticed. "You put in sedum. A good idea. It looks good in summer and adds color in the fall."

Ian took a sip of water, then grinned. "That's what Luther told me. Said it was one of your standbys."

Their food came, and they ate in companionable silence. She could do this. *They* could do it. They could be friends.

On the drive home, she chatted away. Small talk wasn't usually her forte, but she made an effort to keep things light. When he dropped her off, she waved goodbye and went straight into the house. She didn't stand to watch him drive out of sight.

She walked to the sunroom and stared out at the lake. *Shit, that had been hard.* They'd pulled it off, and it would get better with time. But being friends sure as hell wasn't going to be easy, and they'd better not try it too often.

Chapter 27

Her heart wasn't into meeting the new guy she'd agreed to have dinner with in Columbus. But if she didn't make herself get out there, meet new people, she'd return to being her hermit self, and Darinda would hurt her. So would Grams and Keavin.

She parked Gerty a block away, so that her date wouldn't see her beat-up pickup, and she walked to the trendy restaurant where she'd met Aaron. It must be the place men chose to impress women, not that she cared. She just wanted to survive yet another blind date. She scanned the outdoor tables for a man in a teal shirt with a white tie. When she spotted him and started toward him, she looked at the surrounding tables and saw Lily leaning forward to share quips with Aaron.

She froze and Aaron looked up and spotted her. He looked like someone had dumped cold water on him. Lily turned to see what he was staring at and saw Tessa. Her face fell.

Tessa didn't know how to react. What should she do? Point at Lily and make a scene? What would that accomplish? Instead, she walked past them and went to join the man who was waiting for her. He didn't look anything like his picture. He was at least twenty years older. White circled his finger where his wedding band usually sat. He said, "Well, looks like I hit the jackpot. You're lovely."

When the waiter came to take their drink orders, he looked at the man, confused.

Tessa sighed. "Does he usually bring his wife here?"

The waiter looked at the man, not sure how to answer.

Tessa shook her head. "Sorry, this was a mistake. I need to go."

The man didn't argue with her, but as she walked away, Aaron hurried to catch up. Lily was no longer with him. "I didn't think I'd see you here again."

"Obviously. Neither did Lily."

"I feel bad about this. I liked you. I didn't mean . . ."

"Yes, you did. Let's just leave it at that." She kept walking, and he didn't follow.

She turned over one thought after another on the way home. Should she tell Ian? How could she *not* tell him? No one appreciated the bearer of bad news. Would he hate her? But by the time she got home, it was late. She felt frazzled. She decided she'd tell him in the morning, after she'd had time to think of the right words, the right approach.

In the morning, she called him. His voice sounded strained. "Come on over," he said. "I've had a long night."

So had she.

When she got there, she was surprised to see Lily. It was a weekday. She should be off somewhere, traveling the globe. Lily gave her a tight smile. "You're always going to be my nemesis, aren't you? You're never going to go away."

Tessa blinked. "Excuse me? I live here, remember?"

Lily turned to Ian. "I cheated on you. Tessa caught me. She was coming to warn you that I saw another man."

The color drained from Ian's face. He looked lost, confused. "That's why you got here so late last night? Why you've been in such a bad mood?"

"I didn't want to talk about it then. I needed to think it through."

Ian stared. "You cheated on *me*, and it put *you* in a bad mood?"

"I didn't sleep with him."

Ian glared at Tessa. "What the hell happened?"

Lily sagged, as if someone had let the air out of her. "I don't like it here. I like you, but I hate Mill Pond."

"We talked about the lodge. We made the decision together."

"I just wanted you to get it out of your system, so we could move on."

Ian went very still. "It was my dream. You knew that. Why agree to marry me?"

"Look at you. Every other woman wants you. You're rich, handsome, funny—I didn't want to lose you."

Ian looked as though he'd been sucker-punched. A coldness pumped through Tessa's veins. She remembered how much it hurt when she found Gary with Sadie, when she'd realized she hadn't been enough for him.

Ian blinked. He didn't know what to say. He looked confused. "Why tell me to sleep with Tessa if you wanted me for yourself?"

"Because you wanted to, I could tell."

"And it wouldn't have bothered you?"

She hung her head. "I didn't think so at the time, but it wouldn't have worked. I get too jealous of Tessa. Even my damned friends liked her."

Tessa hugged herself, stunned. Lily was jealous of *her*?

Lily watched her reaction and nodded. "I've never been so bitchy to anyone, but you make me feel so inadequate. I know I'm shallow, but I'm fun, and I'm usually nice, and I'm good at my job."

Ian's shoulders sagged. "But you hate it here."

Lily held out her hands in defeat. "I don't fit in. I never will. I don't belong in Mill Pond."

"So you cheated."

"I thought if maybe I had fun on the side, I wouldn't mind not having it here."

Ian shook his head. "I feel like such an idiot."

Lily let out a long breath. She walked to the French doors that looked out over the sweeping back lawn to the lake. "I kept trying to be someone I'm not for you. I told you to buy the resort, hoping you wouldn't like running it, and you'd hire someone to oversee it while you made money in New York. I should have been honest. You can't fit a round peg in a square hole."

Ian looked at her blankly. "We're done, aren't we?"

"We sure as hell are, and it really hurts."

Tessa glanced at Ian. He had the same look of denial she knew she'd had when she'd walked out on Gary. He needed time alone to gather up the pieces and put things in place. "Are you going to be okay?"

Ian nodded. He didn't move and he didn't comment.

Tessa turned on her heel to leave. "I'm sorry," she said to both of them. On the drive home, she couldn't get the image of Ian, stunned and hurt, out of her mind. It would take him a while to heal, she knew. Hopefully, he'd be braver than she was. He wouldn't retreat from the world and hide.

Chapter 28

The bakery had lines of customers on Friday, and every person wanted to talk about Ian. The news had spread through Mill Pond faster than a flash flood.

"That girl was going to marry him and still see her other fella," Iris Clinger hissed, scandalized. "And the poor boy believed every word she told him. If she wasn't ready to settle down, she should have said so."

Leona chimed in. "One of my regular perm customers saw her in Columbus with someone."

The whole day darted from one bit of gossip to the next until, by the time Tessa turned the shop sign to CLOSED, she and Grams both had headaches.

Tessa started to the kitchen. "Want a couple of aspirin before you leave? I could use some."

"Don't mind if I do." Grams followed her and poured them each a glass of water. When Tessa tapped two pills out for her, Grams sighed. "This has been one sucky week, hasn't it?"

"I've had better." Tomorrow could very well be more of the same.

"Want to come to my place for supper tonight? Miguel always makes plenty of food. We're having enchiladas."

"Oh, Grams, you're the best. You know that, right? But I'd rather hide out and feel sorry for myself."

"Can't say that I blame you." Grams gave her a sideways look. "Of course, all this fuss means that Ian's free. Have you thought of that?"

"This mess will probably make things worse between us. He won't trust women again for a while."

Grams patted her arm. "You've waited this long, kid. Give the boy a little space and see what he does. Ian's worth it."

"You know how it goes, I was there when he hit bottom, and that stains everything. We'll never have what we did before. In his mind, I'll be forever connected to the Lily debacle."

"Maybe. Maybe not. He might need a shoulder to cry on, and you have strong shoulders, kiddo."

"Yeah, that's me—Miss Dependability. Rebounds don't work. I'd just be a step to the next woman." Tessa grimaced at her bitter tone. "Sorry. I'm in a mood."

"You know what?" Grams looked at the empty glass cases. They'd regularly refilled them during the day, so the cooler was empty, too. "I think everyone in town came to buy baked goods today. We've sold out. I say we don't open tomorrow. We take Saturday off and let the gossip die down."

Tessa stared. "I've never taken a Saturday off."

"Then it's about time you did. I'll spread the word in town. I'll tell everyone you have a case of the faints."

"The faints?"

"When a frail female's emotions have been overloaded. I'll tell everyone you're devastated that Lily stole your true love in Columbus."

"Aaron? Grams!" But Tessa was laughing. She didn't want to face more people tomorrow, more questions. She shrugged. "Let's do it. I could use a break. So could you."

"Atta girl! I knew you had a little bit of naughty in you." Grams started for the door. "I'll see you next Thursday."

Tessa felt like a rebel as she turned on music and finished cleaning the shop. She went to the computer in her office and put up a message on the shop's Facebook page:

Closed this Saturday due to unforeseen circumstances.

Then she laughed at herself, locked up, and walked to the lake. She was sitting on its shoreline, gazing at the water, when her cell phone rang.

"Where are you? The bakery's closed, isn't it?"

Tessa frowned. She knew that voice. "Lily?"

"Yeah, I know, the last person you want to hear from. But I'm sitting on your porch, and I've told Ian I'm here. I'm not going to his place to get my things. We'd end up rehashing everything. So you'd better get here, or I swear, I'll hurt him."

"You're small. He's big."

"Not *that* kind of hurt, but I know every button of his to push. And I'll do it if I have to."

Could this day get any better? "I was already in the middle of this once."

"Well, you still are, aren't you? So get here."

Lily thought she could play hardball with her. *Well, bring it on!* "I'm on my way." But it wasn't to referee. The girl didn't have the balls to face Ian alone, but that wasn't Tessa's problem. The minute she rounded the front porch, though, there was the sound of tires crunching in the driveway. Oh, damn. This was going to get ugly.

Tessa curled her hands into fists. Ian slammed his car door and stomped toward them. If he breathed fire, it wouldn't surprise her. He looked mad enough. Lily stood near the door, her expression mutinous. Tessa didn't stop to talk to either of them, just unlocked the door, and motioned them inside.

Lily stalked through the front room, past the kitchen, and into the sunroom. Ian took a chair across the room from her. Tessa pulled a wicker rocker halfway between them and to the side, out of the line of fire.

Lily started. "This is all your fault, Ian. You weren't honest with yourself. Or me."

If Ian's expression could grow darker, it did. Tessa expected smoke to come out his ears. "And how did I cause this?" His voice was low, menacing.

Lily squared her shoulders. "When we first met, I told you that I wanted to travel and play my entire life."

"You were an otter." His words were clipped. "You meant to play in the water and eat seafood forever. I remember."

She blinked and brushed at her eyes. "See? That's the thing about you. You're so damned wonderful."

He glowered. "Apparently, not wonderful enough."

"But you are! That's the thing. And I'm wonderful, too. We're just not right for each other."

He sighed. "I don't really want to go through all this again. I'll just hire someone to pack up all your things and send them to whatever address you give me."

She glared. "I'm not living with Aaron. We had dinner together."

"Fine. I'll send them to your apartment."

She blinked back tears. "Please. Don't hate me, Ian. I wanted to be what you wanted. I really did, but I can't."

"I get it." His voice was rough. "You could have been honest, though."

Lily took a deep breath. "The truth is, you love Tessa. You don't want to admit it, but you do. Don't blow it because of stupid pride."

He didn't answer, and Lily pushed herself to her feet. She looked at Tessa. "If he ever gets over himself, have a great life together. You're perfect for him." Then Lily walked to the door and let herself out.

Tessa sat for a minute, not sure what to do.

Then Ian stood, too. He ran a hand through his black hair, still furious. "I have to go. I'm sorry. I'm a mess. I need to think."

Tessa nodded. She understood, and she'd been right. Lily wasn't going to bring them together. She was going to hammer the last nail in their coffin.

Chapter 29

Tessa slept in on Saturday, something she hadn't done in years. Then she took a long shower, pulled on her robe again instead of getting dressed, and looked at herself in the bedroom mirror. Pitiful. It would be nice if water could wash misery down the drain, but it didn't. She trudged to the kitchen and poured herself a cup of coffee. Staring out the window, she couldn't say what she saw. Her life felt blank, empty.

Someone pounded on the door, and she grimaced. If some customer thought she'd go to the barn and dig out a frozen dessert for him, he was mistaken. She whipped the door open and stared. Ian stood there. Stubble covered his chin. His dark hair looked mussed. His shirt was buttoned on a diagonal, one buttonhole off.

She blinked, unsure what to say. Finally, she motioned toward the kitchen. "I have coffee. Want some?"

"No."

She studied his expression. He looked all wound up, ready to burst. "What do you want?"

"I want you."

She stared. "Excuse me?"

"When I found out about Lily, part of me felt betrayed. But the other part of me kept thinking, *good, now I don't have to marry her. I can have Tessa.*"

"Me?"

"Lily was right. I've never wanted anything more in my whole life."

"But Lily . . ."

"Made me laugh, we had great times together. And then I met you."

Her heart started hammering in her chest. Her ears buzzed. She was having a hard time concentrating. "You were going to marry her."

He nodded. "Because I asked her and she said yes. But we were both wrong, both of us. We were so stupid."

Tessa tugged at her hair, pulling it behind her ears. He reached out to touch it. Then their gazes locked, and Ian pushed through the door, slammed it behind him, and crushed her to the wall, his lips grinding against hers.

A well of hunger yawned open, and she met his passion with her own.

When his hand slid beneath her light, summer robe to cradle her breast, she gasped and tensed. Her entire body quivered with need. His thumb teased her nipple, and fire shot through her veins, quickening her senses. Every pore prayed for a caress.

She tilted her head, offering her throat to him. As he nibbled his way up and down her neck, her insides shivered. She started undoing his shirt buttons. Was his skin as smooth and firm as she'd fantasized it to be? A groan escaped her. He was all that and more. She couldn't stop touching.

He bent his head, and his lips grazed the tops of her breasts. She sucked in a breath and arched her back. He ran his tongue over her nipple. Shock waves of want jettisoned through her. When was the last time she'd enjoyed a man's touch? A flood of desire washed away her control, and she tugged at the belt on her robe, pushing the fabric out of his way. One hand held a breast while his mouth claimed the other. A moan ripped from her throat, and she thrust her hips forward. She ripped at his shirt until he shrugged out of it, then her fingers moved to the zipper on his jeans. He undid those and let them drop to the floor. His undershorts followed, and she cupped his ass in her hands. Firm. Rounded. Heaven.

His fingers lowered, exploring the hollows of her abdomen, then moving to her hips, her inner thighs, and then finding warmth and wetness. Her breath stilled. She swore the blood stopped pumping through her veins. Her entire being focused on the movement of his fingers and her pent-up need. Desire built inside her, stoked by want, passion, sensations that refused to be denied. And then he stopped.

Her eyes flew open and she stared at him. He kicked his shoes and pants aside, lifted her in his arms, and stalked to her bedroom. He lowered her on the mattress and sprawled over her, his knees between her legs. And then his head lowered and he nipped at her breasts, his hands roamed her body, and his fingers found her place of need. When her hips came off the bed, he entered her, and their desire found a rhythm. Thrust for thrust, they matched each other. Tessa's skin burned, the heat rising within her. She gripped Ian's shoulders, digging her nails into his skin. She bit her bottom lip and moaned. Then every part of her tensed, ready. They came at the same time.

When the shivers left her, she bit her bottom lip. "Oh, boy."

Ian laughed. "I've had better responses."

"What have we done?"

"We've made it official. I want you. Marry me."

She gaped.

He lowered his lips, and his kisses skimmed her eyes, her cheeks. "I love every inch of you. I love your stubborn chin." He stopped to kiss there. "I love your long throat." He kissed that, too. "Your creamy breasts." More kisses. "Your beautiful body, your strong thighs, your . . ."

She didn't hear the rest. But when they finished, she knew she was loved.

He rolled off of her and nestled close to her side. "Marry me, Tessa."

He'd made her miserable, spending time with Lily. She should put up some kind of battle, not cave in so easily, but she sighed. "Oh, what the hell?"

"Is that a yes?"

"Yes."

He wrapped his arms around her, pulling her close. "It's official then. Let's make it fast."

"No big wedding?"

"Do you want one?"

"No."

"Then the justice of the peace as soon as the paperwork's official."

She nodded. That's all she had the energy to do. All of her senses were concentrating on Ian's body, next to hers. This time, to celebrate, they took their time, each determined to be thorough. Most of Saturday passed as they made up for lost time, but when they finished, they were no longer good friends or neighbors. They were one.

Chapter 30

Tessa and Kayla finished adding the last touches to tiny cream puffs to make them look like swans. Then Tessa gathered up the meringue kiss cookies, bite-sized tarts, and truffles they'd made to add to the delivery boxes.

"I'll be back in a little bit." Tessa left Kayla to start the Boston Cream pies for the lodge's supper menu. She drove to Ian's to find him waiting for her. He hugged her shoulders before he grabbed the top few boxes to carry to the kitchen.

"What did you bring today?" He lifted a lid.

She opened the rest of the boxes to show him, and he grinned his approval. "Did you make any extra for the owner?"

"I saved a few for us tonight."

His chocolate-brown eyes glittered. "You still haven't told me what we're having for supper."

"It's a surprise."

His eyebrows rose. "What's the appropriate menu for finding true love? Tuna casserole? Hamburger and beans?"

She pressed herself against him. "I went with lobsters."

His expression turned mushy. "That good, huh?"

"Memorable."

He tipped her chin upward and bent his head. His kiss left her breathless. "I never thought I'd get this lucky."

"I'll keep reminding you of that."

He pulled her closer. "You don't need to."

Luther swept into the room and grimaced. "Enough already. Save it for the bungalow. I need you to okay the new flower beds out front."

Ian laughed and released her. "Work calls. I'll see you later tonight."

Tessa gave Luther a wave and started back to her place. She chuckled as she parked by the barn. Luther had better enjoy himself while he could. Soon, he'd be getting up all hours of the night with a baby.

A baby. She tilted her head, considering the possibility, but then pushed it aside. A smile curved her lips. She and Ian had lots of time.

Please turn the page for an exciting sneak peek of
Judi Lynn's next Mill Pond romance
OPPOSITES DISTRACT
coming in July 2016 wherever e-books are sold!

Chapter 1

Harmony Meyer listened to the pleasing male voice on her GPS. She was getting close to Lakeview Stables, Ian and Tessa's resort. Fields blanketed with snow spread out on both sides of the highway, the banks close to two feet high, but the road was plowed and decent to travel. The weather had been mild all through December, but once January shook its wintry head the snow had started. At least she didn't have to fight ice or she'd have stayed home rather than risk life and limb.

At a stop sign in the middle of nowhere she noticed two horses in a fenced-in pasture. One of them looked satiny and honey-colored. The other had brown spots on white, just like her neighbor's rat terrier back home in New York. Mist billowed from the horses' nostrils, and Harmony smiled when they turned to race to a nearby barn. A man crossed a driveway toward the big red building. Their owner? Her thoughts wandered until the sharp sound of a horn jerked her gaze behind her. A forbidding, dark SUV with tinted windows lurked close to her bumper. Damn, when did he get there?

With a casual wave to the driver behind her, Harmony returned her attention to the road and followed the route her nice GPS man told her. She frowned when the black SUV took every turn she did. Should she be concerned? What if the driver was a serial killer who followed innocent young women on Indiana back roads to scare them half to death? She snickered. She was far from innocent. Besides, she'd taken a self-defense class and carried pepper spray. Too bad for him.

When she turned into the wide lane that led to the main lodge, the big black beast of an SUV did the same. The hairs prickled on the back of her neck. What were the odds two people would arrive at a nearly deserted resort at the same time on the same day? It was the middle of January, the resort's dead time. Her friend Tessa Lawrence had guaranteed she'd have the place mostly to herself. Harmony parked near the front door. Before she could reach it, Tessa stepped outside to greet her.

"Harmony!" Tessa's tangle of copper hair glowed in the sunlight. Her lips curved in a smile. A tall, gorgeous man with black hair and a lean build stood beside her. Must be the new hubby.

Harmony looked him over and gave a low laugh. Scrumptious. She shook her head at her friend. "No wonder you ditched your single days."

Tessa made the introductions. "Harmony, my husband, Ian. Ian, my writer buddy, Harmony. We always go to the same writers' conferences and room together. Then we stay over a few days for sightseeing."

Ian grinned. Major heartthrob. "So, you're the one who writes about witches and werewolves. Tess says you write romances like hers, but scarier."

"And a hell of a lot sexier." Harmony gave Tessa a considering look. "But that might change now that she's married."

A car door slammed and Ian turned his gaze to the dark SUV. A hulk of a man—maybe a body builder—carting two heavy suitcases with ease, walked toward them. Ian grinned. "Brody!"

Tessa opened her arms to greet him. "Harmony, this is Ian's big brother. He owns a construction company, but since business is slow this time of year he came to help Ian divide the west wing of the inn into four more rooms."

Brody's hair was as dark as his brother's, but his eyes were a cool, smoky gray instead of warm brown, and his build bulged with muscle. Intimidating.

She straightened her shoulders. No one would intimidate her ever again. Brody studied her quickly and dismissed her. Must not like blondes with blue eyes . . . and attitude.

Harmony raised her chin. To each his own. Probably just as well, though. She hadn't come here to flirt. If she didn't write like a mad woman she'd miss her deadline. Unthinkable. She'd work twenty-four hours a day if she had to.

Damn her landlord. He'd taken it into his head to get rid of the old boiler and redo her building's entire heating system. In January. Go figure. Lots of dust and noise. Not conducive to concentrating and letting her subconscious untangle plot lines. She tried going to a coffee house to work on her laptop, but she was too nosy, got distracted by watching people come and go. So Tessa had suggested she come here. For free. Tessa wrote during the winter months, too. They'd eat supper together every night and yak together like they did at conferences. How could Harmony refuse?

Brody shrugged his broad shoulders. "You guys can make small talk out here in the cold if you want to, but I'd rather go inside where it's warm." He stalked away.

Ian turned to her. "Sorry. I should have offered to get your bags while you and Tess wait in the lobby. I'll be there soon." He stretched out his hand for her keys and strode toward her Jeep. His boots crunched on the salted drive.

Harmony stopped to admire the lodge—a flagstone house with white trim and a red tin roof. It stood three stories high in the center with a wing off each end and red double doors in its center. "No wonder Ian loved this place the minute he saw it."

A golf course stretched to the east of the parking lot, and stables and paddocks to the west. The lake lay in back with log cabins dotted along the east shore.

Tessa glowed with pride. "Sam, the previous owner, kept the exterior in great shape, but nothing had been done inside for over a decade. It needed lots of work. We're pretty proud of how it turned out." She led Harmony into the warm, comforting lobby with gleaming, maple floors and high, beamed ceilings.

Harmony glanced upward with a grin. "No bats?" Tessa had told her the story of Ian and his nocturnal visitor.

Tessa laughed and shook her head. "Only the one and that was enough." She pointed to hooks along the inside wall. "If you want to leave your coat here, you can. Then it's handy."

Brody had dropped his suitcases on the floor near the front desk, tossed his wool coat on a hook, and sat on one of the plush, brown leather sofas in front of the fireplace. He stretched his long legs before him. His gaze fastened on Tessa and he smiled. "How's life with my brother?"

She went to perch on a forest-green chair across from him and motioned for Harmony to take the seat next to hers. "I still kinda like the guy."

Brody laughed. "That's good. The family signed you up for life. We don't do returns."

When Ian draped his jacket over the back of the couch and sat next to his brother, Harmony had a chance to study them more thoroughly. Both men would turn heads. Tall and dark-haired, they exuded maleness.

Ian motioned toward her suitcases. "When you're ready I'll show you to your room. I put you on the top floor, far enough from our project that we shouldn't disturb you."

Brody turned his attention on her again. "I noticed your license plate. You're from New York?"

She nodded. "The Finger Lakes region. That's why I drive a Jeep. Winters can get serious there."

"I live near Ithaca too."

She frowned. How odd that they'd both traveled to the same spot in Indiana from the same area in New York. Fate? Nah. No stars were stupid enough to throw her and Brody together. He made her nervous, he was so intense.

The dark brow rose again. "If Ian had told me you were coming here, I could have offered you a ride." He sounded as appalled by the idea as she felt. She grinned. He could have, but it wouldn't have happened.

She gave her head a quick shake and crossed her fingers. "I'm staying a month until my apartment building's finished. You probably won't be here that long."

He stared. "Actually, I will. Ian's project is going to take a while. This is the only time I can help him. I go to our parents' place for the Christmas holidays, and then business picks up in March."

She didn't hide her lack of enthusiasm that well. Why should she? He wasn't exactly doing somersaults about enduring her company. "We probably won't see that much of each other. I'll be at my laptop all day."

Tessa beamed at the two of them. "Actually, you two will be coming to our house for supper most nights. That way, we'll get to spend some time with you."

Harmony's shoulders sagged; Brody's stiffened.

Oh, goodie! She stifled her sarcasm. If only she were as *nice* as Tessa. She'd make an effort. She'd be the epitome of charm. They'd eat together, then Ian would drag Brody off to talk about guy things, and she and Tessa would cozy up somewhere to yak. Harmony was fully capable of civilized behavior when the need arose.

The front door opened and a woman with two children interrupted their conversation. Harmony stared, surprised. The woman had dyed black hair pulled up in a clip, a nose ring, and more tattoos than Harmony could count. She looked out of place in this rustic setting.

"Hi, I'm Paula, Ian's cook."

Before Harmony could respond, the little girl—maybe five, with black hair like her mother's—ran straight to her and wrapped her in a hug. "You look just like Princess Elsa in *Frozen*."

"*Frozen*?" Harmony blinked.

Paula laughed. "You must not know Disney kids' movies. Bailey's in love with all things about Arendelle and the two princesses."

Bailey plopped on Harmony's lap and said, "This is so cool! You look like Elsa and Tessa looks like Merida from *Brave*."

Harmony made a mental note to look up both of the movies on her laptop. Merida must have wild red hair if she looked like Tessa.

"Move it, kid!" Paula motioned for her daughter to scoot toward their apartment in the inn's east wing. Harmony had heard a lot about Paula and her kids from Tessa—all good. When Paula's son, maybe ten, got close to Harmony, he stopped to look her up and down, too.

"Do you like kids?" he asked.

Oh Lord, what was she getting herself into at this resort? She gave him a level stare. "Why? You aren't going to put a toad in my coffee cup, are you?"

His eyes went wide, surprised by her answer. "Mom would ground me."

Harmony smiled. "Then we'll get along great."

"Mom says you write books. You must like them."

Okay, she hadn't seen that coming. "I have a few favorites."

"Would you read to us?"

"My books?" Her voice rose. Her vampires tended to be a bit horny, not good reading material for kids.

"Harry Potter."

She pursed her lips, considering. She'd never cracked one of those books. Probably missed out on a cultural milestone. "What time? I have to hit my page quotas every day before I do anything." But after she wrote for five or six hours, her brain went to hell. She was lucky if she could think of two-syllable words. A break would be good for her.

"Before supper?" He narrowed his eyes, waiting for her answer.

She'd be shot by then, brain dead. "Hell, why not?"

The boy smiled. "I'm Aiden. The book has long chapters."

"Tough luck. I can give you thirty to forty minutes. I have a short attention span." Especially when it came to kids. Harmony looked at Paula. "Is that all right with you?"

Paula's grin widened. Mimicking her, she said, "Hell, why not?"

Ian laughed. "I have a feeling you guys are going to get along fine."

"Just come up and knock on my door when you're ready," Harmony said. "That will help keep me on a schedule. When I start writing, I lose track of time."

Paula herded her kids to their apartment, and Harmony let out a sigh. She turned to see Brody studying her once again. She grimaced. "I know. I probably shouldn't cuss in front of kids."

"You made that kid a promise. You're going to keep it, right?" His voice sounded flinty, judgmental.

Harmony struggled with her temper, but didn't tamp it down completely. She gave him a look, her voice equally sharp. "I don't make promises I don't keep...to anyone. Why do you think I came here? I'm trying to keep my promise to my editor and get my damned book to him on time."

He raised his eyebrows. "You should have red hair like Tessa. It sounds like you have a temper."

"It's different. Blondes only hiss when we're provoked."

"If you say so. The blondes I've met are frivolous."

"Then you meet the wrong ones," she snapped.

A smile tugged at his lips. "I'll have to remedy that."

Oh, crap. What had she done?

Chapter 2

Ian carried Harmony's bags to the third floor and opened the door to her room. "Tessa insisted you have this one because she said it was your favorite color."

Harmony raised a hand to her lips. The room took her breath away. "It's beautiful." The walls were painted a soft apricot and the gleaming wood floors were dotted with braided rugs. A mini-fridge nestled under a small counter with a coffee pot. White curtains framed a wide window that looked out over the lake at the back of the property. Right now a layer of ice covered it. In the distance she could see people ice fishing. A desk sat before the window and two overstuffed chairs in the corner invited settling in with a book. A fluffy white bedspread was made even cozier with a peach-colored throw angled over the footboard.

Ian grinned. "I'm glad you like it. Tessa thought you'd want to get settled. Brody will drive you to our house for supper at six."

"He's staying in the inn? Tessa said he was staying at your house."

"We invited him to. He didn't think that was right when Tessa invited you and you were staying here."

"Does he always do what he thinks is right? He never bends the rules, even to spend more time with you guys?"

Ian laughed. "Brody's the oldest kid of our brood. I have two older sisters, Bridget and Maeve. I was the baby. Brody felt it was his duty to keep us in line."

"The authoritarian. I get it."

"We made his life hell." Ian turned to leave. "Tessa said to tell you that she made gumbo for supper. Said that was guaranteed to get you there on time."

Harmony licked her lips. "One of my favorites. Tessa and I were on panels together at a romance conference in New Orleans. I came away craving Creole, Cajun, and all things spicy."

When Ian left, she reached for the case that held her laptop. She could put her clothes away later, but while she had an hour or two and her mind was fresh, she could slip in a little writing time. She kicked off her shoes and wiggled her stockinged feet. Time to get comfortable and settle in.

She'd written the book's hook and the first six chapters, but hadn't taken the time to edit them. She'd introduced Serefina, the witch protagonist, and her future romantic interest, Luxar—a vampire. They'd each been fighting an unknown enemy in their city. The reader knew they both battled Torrid, and soon, they'd collide to work together to save Portside.

She was wading through rewrites when a knock on her door interrupted her. She glanced at the clock. Holy shit. 5:30. She pushed the save button on her computer and went to see who was there. Aiden wouldn't show up for story time the first day she got here, would he?

Brody glowered down at her. "Looks like Tessa was right and you got lost in your writing world. She phoned and asked me to check on you."

He made it sound like an accusation. She shrugged. "It's what I do. I don't usually stop until my stomach growls. I'm not used to a schedule."

"But you do try to be considerate of friends and hostesses?"

This guy could be a real dick. She crossed her arms. "I had my phone alarm set for 5:40."

She barely got the words out when the alarm went off. "Oh, baby, baby, my baby, baby" sang through the room.

Brody raised his eyebrows. "Whatever gets your attention."

She ground her teeth, then frowned at him. "You cleaned up." He still wore his worn, comfortable jeans, but he'd changed into a button-down shirt and sweater. He'd be yummy if he weren't such a sourpuss.

He looked her up and down. "I guess I didn't need to bother." She hadn't changed out of her driving clothes—faded jeans with a few rips in the right thigh area and a baggy sweater. Her hair was still pulled back in a low ponytail.

"I didn't know gumbo meant a formal dinner." She yanked at the scrunchie that held her hair, letting loose waves cascade past her shoulders.

Brody stared, then shook his head. "No matter. Shall we? It's time to go." In the lobby, he waited for her to shrug into her winter coat and then walked with her to his SUV. She wasn't short, but the step-up to get into the passenger seat was more exertion than she was used to. He gave a grim smile, enjoying her effort. He'd be surprised to know how much she walked back home. She was in good shape, whether he thought so or not, damn the man!

When she fastened her seatbelt, he shut the door and circled the vehicle to slide behind the steering wheel. On the drive to Tessa's, she mentally calculated how much time they'd have to spend together. Not all that much. Her stay here looked better.

Harmony grinned from ear to ear when they pulled into the driveway. The wide bungalow was as charming as she'd pictured it. White, with green shutters and flower boxes, it looked warm and welcoming. She reached for the door handle, but Brody shook his head. What now? He walked around the SUV to open her door for her. She stared at him. "Are you for real?"

"I am, but I think you've lived with vampires and werewolves too long to remember some of the social norms."

"No one opens doors for women anymore."

Brody shrugged. "They should."

A thick layer of snow blanketed the yard and the house's roof. It looked like something on a Christmas card—inviting and cozy, especially since the sidewalks were cleared. Harmony hurried up the path.

Tessa threw open the front door before they reached it and pulled Harmony inside. "I can't believe you came. I'm stuck on a scene in chapter eleven. Where are you in your book?"

Ian rolled his eyes and waited for his brother to join them. "Tessa promised not to talk writing during supper."

Brody smiled. "I'm sure she keeps her promises, just like Harmony claims she does."

"I heard that!" Harmony threw him a dirty glance over her shoulder before the two women took off for the kitchen together.

Ian grinned. "You got in trouble."

"Yeah, I'm worried now." Brody hung his pea coat on the coat tree by the front door, carefully wiped his feet on the welcome mat, then trailed behind them. He sniffed as he went. "Mmm, something smells good."

Harmony twirled in a happy circle in the kitchen. "I can't believe you remembered. We ate this together in New Orleans when we skipped out for a few hours between panels."

Tessa pointed to the oven. "Do you remember what we had for dessert?"

"You didn't!"

Tessa opened the oven door a crack. "Bread pudding with whiskey sauce."

Harmony hugged herself.

Brody shook his head. "For how thin they are both of these women *really* love food."

"And you don't?" Ian opened the refrigerator to grab a bottle of wine and two bottles of beer.

Brody accepted one. "That's Mom's fault. She cooked a meal every night, and every meal came with dessert."

"Then this will feel just like home." Ian motioned for him to help carry heavy pots to the round cherry wood table. Trivets waited for them. Tessa sat across from Ian, Brody across from Harmony. Oh, good, Brody could watch her eat. When they were all seated, they dug in.

Tessa's bungalow lived up to everything Harmony expected. White cupboards lined three walls. Granite countertops provided plenty of work space, and the oak floors looked worn and homey.

Ian pointed his spoon at Brody. "Fill me in on what everyone's up to at home."

Brody told him about their parents and sisters. "Maeve's youngest boy...."

Ian interrupted. "How old is Connor?"

"Four now, he broke his arm after Christmas. Got a sled from Santa and went down the wrong hill."

Tessa winced. "Is he all right?" She glanced at Harmony. Harmony had broken her arm as a kid when her brother pushed her off their backyard swing set.

"Kids heal fast, but he hates his cast. Itches. It's a good thing Maeve can work on her bookkeeping from home."

"And Bridget?" Ian glanced at Tessa's copper hair. "My sister's the woman who gave redheads a bad name. What a temper!"

"She's fine. Likes her students this year. No one's blown up the

Chemistry lab yet." Brody paused for a second. Voice low, he said, "Cecily remarried on New Year's Day."

Ian fumbled his fork. "The bitch talked another man into marrying her?"

Harmony felt her eyes go wide. She wasn't good at hiding her feelings. Tessa turned to her and whispered, "Brody's ex. Ugly divorce."

Harmony had wondered. He looked to be about forty and didn't wear a ring. Either he'd always been a woman-hater or he'd recently become one.

Tessa reached over to touch Brody's hand. "I'm sorry. That had to be hard for you."

He grunted. "Not really. They'll probably make it to happy-ever-after. She married someone a lot older with loads of money. I heard he loves to dote on her."

"Everything on her bucket list," Ian said.

Harmony asked, "Is she a blonde?" The man certainly had a low opinion of them. Maybe Cecily was the reason.

Ian answered. "No, a ball-buster brunette." He obviously didn't like Brody's ex.

Harmony raised her hands in defeat. "I guess females in general don't cut it. Blondes are bubble-heads, brunettes bust balls, and redheads have fiery tempers. Brody likes Tessa, though. So maybe a girl has to have copper hair to pass inspection."

Brody quirked an eyebrow. "Why? Are you interested in giving it a go?"

"Me? No, just asking out of curiosity."

Brody focused on her. "Have you been married? In a serious relationship?"

Those smoky-gray eyes made her squirm. "Not my thing. I get distracted too easily."

"No heartbreak in your past?" he persisted.

Tessa glanced her way. She looked uncomfortable. "She wouldn't allow that."

"None at all?" Brody sounded surprised.

Harmony shrugged. "A drummer once stole a carton of cigarettes from me when he left before breakfast, but that was good. I meant to give up smoking anyway."

His lips curled in a half-smile. "So you've stayed single out of convenience, and I'm single because I got screwed over."

Convenience? Hardly. More like self-preservation. When you let someone touch your heart, they had the power to control you. "Looks that way." Harmony scooped up a forkful of rice, but he wasn't finished.

"Do you want to find someone someday?"

She shook her head. It was safer to keep people at a distance. Except Tessa. Writing had drawn them together. "I'm happy doing what I do. Why complicate it?" He'd made her curious, though. She couldn't help it. She'd always been nosy, even before she started writing. "You?" she asked.

He nodded. "I want someone who's smart, funny, loves to cook, loves to entertain, and wants to have children."

"That's why you bugged me about my promise to Aiden." The words popped out before she could stop them. When would she learn to be more discreet, to let conversations die that were getting uncomfortable?

"I wanted to have kids. Cecily didn't. She *said* she did, but she kept putting it off."

Smart Cecily. "Kids aren't for me. They're even more bother than a man."

Ian laughed. "Do you have a pet? Anything?"

"I feed pigeons on my window ledge every morning after breakfast."

Brody stared. "And that's enough for you?"

What did he want from her? She could make up a story. She was good at that. She could tell him that she baked cookies to take to the homeless every weekend and that she rescued strays off the street. But she didn't need to impress him, so she might as well be honest. "When I'm lonely, I meet up with friends or go to a bar and sit on a stool next to someone. It works for me."

"One night stands?"

Ian shook his head. "Brody. . . ."

But Harmony didn't mind. Her life wasn't all that exciting. He'd yawn before long. "No, I only need lust when I finish writing a book. Sort of a celebration."

He shook his head, frustrated. "I've never met a woman like you."

"Consider that a blessing." But fair was fair. She told hers. He should tell his. She asked again, "You?"

He grimaced. He was more private than she was, she could tell. "Occasionally."

She gave a knowing nod. "Once in a while, we just need a human touch." She took the last bite of her meal and glanced toward the bread pudding.

Tessa grinned. "You've always had a sweet tooth."

Brody stood to collect dirty dishes and carry them to the sink. Did the freaking man do *everything* right? Ian cleared away the leftovers and brought the bread pudding to the table. Their mom must have trained her boys well. They knew their stuff.

Ian steered the conversation to small talk while they finished up. Then Tessa shooed the men from the kitchen, and she and Harmony rinsed and cleaned so that they could sit at the table, bump heads, and yak writing.

Serious, ready for shop talk, Harmony asked, "So what's the hang-up in chapter eleven?"

"The scene I planned just won't work." Tessa did a quick run-down of her new book, her characters, and where she was stuck.

They brainstormed until Brody wandered out from a back room around ten. "We'd better get back for the night. Ian and I are starting work early tomorrow morning. We have a lot to get done in a month."

Harmony stretched and yawned. "I have a lot to do, too." She bent to hug Tessa. "See you tomorrow. Can I help with anything? Come early to set the table?"

"Nope, I'm enjoying myself. Just show up on time for supper." She raised an eyebrow at Brody. "You'll have to pry her fingers off her keyboard."

"Got it." He held out Harmony's coat for her, then shrugged into his own. When they stepped outside, a wind hit them, blasting off the lake. It picked up snow and pelted it at them.

"Damn, it's cold!" Harmony hustled for the SUV. She hopped in-side and slammed the door before she remembered Brody's rules. The man didn't get to do door duty this time, but he looked mighty relieved when he slid behind the steering wheel. The warmth of the SUV thawed her on the short drive back. He pulled close to the doors of the resort and started to get out, but she was too quick. She dashed out of the car and into the lobby before he could stop her.

She could get used to having a man deliver her almost to the front door, but she'd better not get too comfortable with it. It wouldn't happen at home. She waited inside the lobby for him. He looked surprised to see her when he stepped into the foyer. "I thought you'd zip up to your room."

She grimaced. "I might not be traditional, but I have some manners. Thanks for the ride."

He frowned at her. "Ian told me your favorite color is apricot."

She blinked. Where the hell had that come from? How did this man keep throwing her off balance? "Yeah, I guess it is."

"That's so feminine. You're . . ." He hesitated.

She gave his arm a playful punch. "No worries. I get it. I'm not."

They said their goodnights and went their separate ways. Once in her room, Harmony went to the window to watch white flurries swirl outside. A storm was blowing toward them, intense enough that she couldn't see to the other side of the lake. She closed the blinds and changed into her pajamas. Then she crawled into bed and dragged her laptop with her. She balanced it on the bedspread and finished the rewrites of the chapters she'd been working on, but her thoughts kept drifting to Brody. Had he been hopeful, madly in love when he married his Cecily? And what had she done to him? A reason, Harmony reminded herself, she avoided happily ever after. Because it was a crapshoot whether or not it would work.

Judi Lynn received a Master's Degree from Indiana University as an elementary school teacher after attending the IPFW campus. She taught first, second, and fourth grades for six years before having her two daughters. She loves gardening, cooking, and trying new recipes. Readers can visit her website at http://www.judithpostswritingmusings.com/ and her blog http://writingmusings.com/.